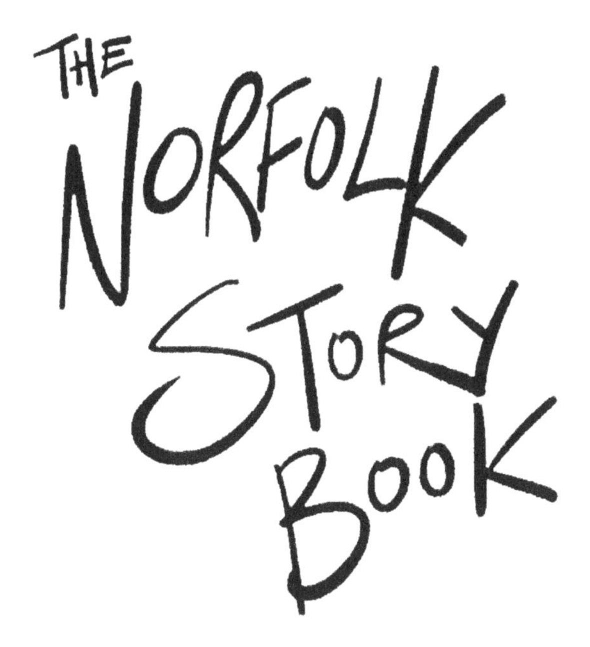

WRITTEN BY

ISABELLE KING

ILLUSTRATED BY
JOHN McKEEVER

First published 2016

The History Press
The Mill, Brimscombe Port
Stroud, Gloucestershire, GL5 2QG
www.thehistorypress.co.uk

British Library Cataloguing in Publication Data.
A catalogue record for this book is available from the British Library.

ISBN 978 0 7509 6792 1

Typesetting and origination by The History Press
Printed in Great Britain

CONTENTS

INTRODUCTION AND THANK YOUS

Isabelle King (© Wolf Marloh Photography)

My first encounter with Norfolk Museums Service was to visit Norwich Castle Museum when I was very little. To this day, I remember being captivated by roaring tigers, spooky dungeons, Egyptian mummies, extraordinary paintings and a castle keep with a well that goes down, down, down …

It was a magical experience that went on to inspire much of my work life. When I was a bit older I undertook work experience at Norwich Castle and learned more about the breadth of the history contained inside its walls. This included having the pleasure of watching plans for the ancient Roman Boudicca exhibition take shape. I went on to participate in the Viking Project in which I worked with groups of children to help create a drama show about these fearsome invaders and did a bit of dressing up myself because, really, who wouldn't leap at the chance to dress up like a Viking?

I loved the way Norfolk Museums Service engaged visitors through drama and imagination and was keen to further develop my involvement as an interpreter in local museums. Gressenhall Farm and Workhouse Museum presented a perfect opportunity for this with the Company of Enactors. I took part in a series of re-enactments called *A Day in the Life of a Workhouse Inmate*. I learned a huge amount about the lives of very poor people, what they ate (which wasn't much) and where they slept (which wasn't comfy) including a trip to the somewhat terrifying punishment cell. Whilst in the punishment cell, I remember one of the Workhouse Interpreters telling me to touch the walls and think of all the people over the generations who had touched the same walls, and imagine what their lives must have been like. This sparked my fascination with objects in relation to people's lives, a theme which I go on to explore in this book.

Before this, I had some life experience to get on with (I was not quite so little at this stage, about medium height). Inspired by my experiences with Norfolk Museums Service, I went on to train as a professional actress, determined to pursue a career which interwove drama with history and education. I trained with National Youth Theatre and at East 15 Acting School, after which followed work with the Young Shakespeare Company, Cambridge Shakespeare Festival, Vienna's English Theatre and some London theatres, as well as various films and voiceover work. Particular highlights included playing a dancing chicken in a children's show and voicing a cat in an animation film. Never a dull moment.

I am also the founder of Books Talk Back: a series of literary events for writers, which I organise and host, and which have gained support from The British Library and Writers' Centre Norwich.

As much as I enjoyed my varied and somewhat chaotic career of cat voices, Shakespearian guises and book events, it had long been a dream of mine to combine this creative work with my enthusiasm for where it all started, with Norfolk Museums Service.

In 2015, when I was something resembling a grown up, I visited Norfolk Collections Centre and found myself mesmerised by the wonderful variety of curious and delightful objects that are in store.

Each story in this book is a work of fiction, inspired by an object featured at Norfolk Collections Centre. I picked seven objects which sparked my imagination and which I thought would have been most appealing to me when I was younger. With help from staff at Norfolk Museums Service, I thoroughly researched each object's history. Then I set each tale in its correct historical context, and imagined the characters, situations and sense of magic which makes up each story, based around what I'd learned about the objects.

The seven objects the book focusses on are: a Snap Dragon, a Mammoth Skull, a Mustard Stamper, St Gregory's Rood Screen, the statue of Samson from the Samson and Hercules duo, a Toffee Guillotine and Caley's Christmas Crackers. All these objects can be seen at Norfolk Collection Centre and the crackers and statue of Samson are now at the Museum of Norwich at the Bridewell. I have loved writing stories about these exciting, iconic items belonging to the place where I grew up – Norfolk.

I have very much enjoyed delving into the fascinating history of each object which has involved multiple visits to Norfolk Collections Centre and the Museum of Norwich at the Bridewell, as well as trips to some of the sites featured in these stories, including St Gregory's Church, Norwich Cathedral and Samson and Hercules House.

A particular highlight in my investigations has been consuming vast quantities of toffee for the Toffee Guillotine story, naturally for serious research purposes. In addition, this book has presented the perfect excuse for me to explore and write about animals of all kinds, from friendly mammoths to beautiful bouncy dogs, a welcome opportunity for an animal enthusiast.

As a performance storyteller, I frequently take part in family events throughout Norfolk Museums Service and absolutely love bringing the stories to life, off the page, in my storytelling sessions which are imaginative, improvised and fun.

All in all, writing this book has been an incredible adventure for me, but it would never have been possible without the fantastic support of the staff at Norfolk Museums Service.

In particular, I would like to give special thanks to the kind and continual support of Wayne Kett and Jamie Everitt at Norfolk Collections Centre, without whom this book would, quite simply, not exist! They helped to choose the objects, they read the stories countless times to ensure they were factually correct, and they organised my very first storytelling session for the book at the Gressenhall Farm and Workhouse's Summer Story Festival, where I told some of the stories in front of the objects from which they were inspired.

I would also like to thank the support of the Chief Curator for the Norfolk Museums Service, Dr John Davies; together with Head of Learning, Colly Mudie; Retail Manager, Maria Wong; Informal Learning Officer, Anna McCarthy; as well as Jenny Caynes and Kate Cooper at the Museum of Norwich at the Bridewell and Cathy Terry at Stranger's Hall.

Finally, I would like to thank the objects themselves! Yes, it is a little odd thanking an object but I've grown rather fond of them. My biggest wish is that, having read the stories, you will visit the museums and see these wondrous things for yourself! The seven featured in this book are far from the only objects on display throughout Norfolk Museums Service. Perhaps next time you visit a Norfolk Museums Service museum you could pick an object which captivates you and write a story about it. Now, let's get lost in some Norfolk magic!

WHAT THE STORY TITLES MEAN

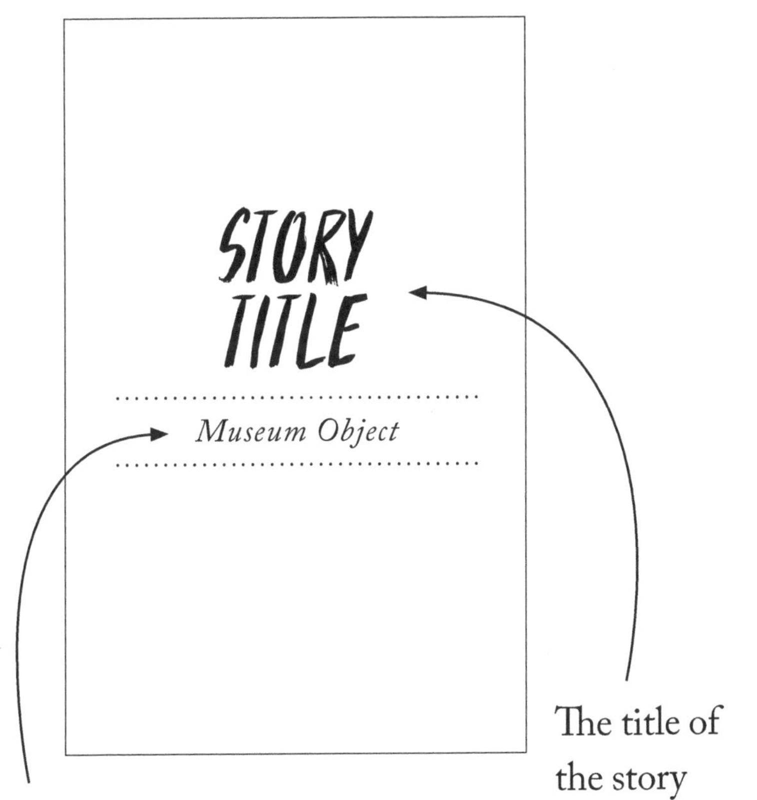
STORY TITLE
Museum Object
The title of the story that you are about to read
This refers to the museum object that inspired the story

ALICE AND THE SNAP DRAGON

Snap Dragon

This story is set a very, very long time ago. So long ago, that the people who lived in this time couldn't even tell the time. That is to say, they didn't have clocks or watches or phones which told them it was seven o'clock in the morning or ten past one in the afternoon and time for lunch. The only way that they could tell the time was to measure the movement of the sun. As soon as it was light it was time for breakfast. As soon as it was dark it was time for bed.

This story all happened in Norwich. Back then it was a very different city to how it is now. It took ages to get anywhere because there were no cars or buses. Instead, people rode horses or simply walked on foot. The streets were very dirty and smelly and, sometimes, so were the people. Nobody had showers in their houses so some people washed wherever they could find water, and some people just didn't wash at all.

There really wasn't much choice as to what you could eat. Most people lived on a diet of plain, boring gruel which filled you up but wasn't very tasty.

Our story begins with a little girl called Alice. Alice lived in Norwich, in this very long time ago, with her Mum, Dad, two brothers, John and Peter, and sister Matilda. The house they lived in was very small, so small that at night-time they all had to share the same bedroom to sleep in. Alice knew that her family were very poor and this was the reason why their house was so small. It got very crowded sometimes, and she generally would have liked a bit more personal space but, on the whole, Alice didn't mind because she loved her family.

One morning Alice woke up feeling very excited. She didn't have an alarm clock to wake her up but she knew that it was morning because the sun was shining through the window of their bedroom and her stomach was rumbling, so it was definitely time for breakfast. On an ordinary day Alice would simply have got up and got on with her day. But today was not an ordinary day. Today was a very special day because today was Guild Day. Guild Day was one of the most magical, most spectacular, most brilliant days of the year.

Once every year, on a bright spring day, many people in the city would get together for a big party on the streets of Norwich. Not just any old party: there would be music and dancing and jollity, yes, but there would also be a theatrical extravaganza; a play with real actors would be put on by a host of people who called themselves The Guild of St George and they would act out the story of St George and the Dragon. It was this play that made Guild Day one of the most magical, most spectacular, most brilliant days of the year because the star of this play was the Norwich Snap Dragon.

If Alice were to describe the Snap Dragon to you, she would tell you that he is a wonderful sight indeed. The first thing you would notice is that he is a very colourful thing; he is covered in scales, some are red, some are green and some glisten from yellow to gold in the sun. He is surprisingly small for a dragon, with a large round belly that looks too heavy for his little legs to carry, but don't be fooled; the Snap Dragon is very nimble on his feet. If you're not careful, he will run up behind you when you're not looking and snap his jaws together to make you jump. Believe me, Alice would say, you don't want to be too close to the Snap Dragon's jaws. He has hundreds of sharp, pointy teeth that look ready to bite, and not only that, he can really breathe fire. Imagine that, a fire-breathing dragon on the streets on Norwich!

This might all sound a bit scary, but Alice would assure you that the Snap Dragon would never hurt anybody; he just likes to give people a bit of a fright. Really, he is a very friendly, playful thing and the fact that he can sometimes be a bit unpredictable is all part of what makes him the most fantastic fun.

Alice didn't know where the Snap Dragon lived or why he chose only to be amongst the people of Norwich on Guild Day. She wished that he would come out and play every day of the year and not just on that one special day. Now, you might have guessed this already, but one of the reasons why Alice was so excited about seeing the Snap Dragon was that she truly believed he was a real live dragon.

That morning, when she thought about the Snap Dragon, Alice got the same feeling she got when she woke up and realised that it was her birthday.

Alice and her siblings were all squashed together in the same bed. She reached over and prodded her brother, Peter, who was lying next to her. 'Peter, Peter, wake up, it's Guild Day.'

Peter grunted and rolled over.

Alice prodded him a few more times for good measure. '*Guild Day!*'

'It's still early Alice,' Peter groaned, 'go back to sleep!'

But Alice did not go back to sleep. Instead, she got up, got dressed and headed straight out of the house. She wanted to see what the world outside looked like on this very special day. Alice stood at the front door and gazed down the road. The world outside did not disappoint.

The streets were already decorated in preparation for Guild Day with bright banners of all the different colours you could think of. Alice ran down the road to get a better look at them. It was so colourful; it seemed to her as though a rainbow had exploded across the street. She got even more excited at the thought of seeing the Snap Dragon later.

Alice ran back to the house and on her way through the front door bumped into Dad.

Alice never really knew what to say to Dad. Dad was always busy and cross and worrying about something. He never wanted to spend any time with Alice and he certainly never wanted to play with her.

Mum had told Alice that the reason Dad was like this was because he was always trying to earn money for the family to live on. The trouble was, Dad didn't have a job. Instead, he did lots of different jobs, some days he did this, some days he did that, and some days he did this and that, but he never knew where his next job was coming from. He was always so busy trying to find work that he didn't have any time for Alice and the rest of the family. Alice did feel sorry for Dad because she knew that having to find work all the time must have been a lot of pressure for him. Still, she couldn't help but wish that he would be less grumpy and would sometimes play with her, or at least say 'good morning' every once in a while.

Alice bowed her head and stayed quiet until Dad brushed past her without a word on his way through the front door. Whenever he left the house early it was because he was going to work. But today was Guild Day and everybody in the city had a day off work. What sort of job could Dad possibly be doing on Guild Day? Alice had no idea, but one thing was clear: Dad wouldn't be coming with them to the Guild Day celebrations. This made Alice very sad, because it was the one day of the year that the family had a chance to all be together.

After breakfast, which was gruel, followed by gruel, with some gruel on top, it was time to go to the celebrations.

Mum rounded up the four children and made sure that they were all looking their best. She made Alice run her fingers through her hair to untangle it, several times, because it had got messy from running on the street.

'You, young lady,' she told Alice, 'always look like a little vagabond.'

Then all the family headed off to Norwich Cathedral, which was where the Guild Day celebrations were starting. Well, all the family except Dad.

Norwich Cathedral was an enormous, great big building, the biggest building that Alice had ever seen. It had pointy turrets sticking out in all directions and some of the turrets were so tall that they swept all the way up to the sky.

Outside Norwich Cathedral the party was in full swing. All around Alice was music and laughter and noise. There were so many people about that Mum made everyone hold hands so as not to get lost.

The crowd had gathered in a ring with a large circle in the middle where the play was about to take place. Alice and her family were right at the back of the crowd and Alice couldn't see what was going on through the people in front of them, so Peter, who was the oldest and quite tall, lifted her up on his shoulders so she could get a better view. When it was time for the play everyone fell silent. Then a man of great importance walked into the space to speak. Alice knew he must have been a man of great importance because, even though everyone around him was smiling, he looked very stern. Men of great importance, she noted, were always too busy being important to look happy.

'People of Norwich,' he said in a loud, booming voice, 'I present to you, the story of St George and the Dragon!'

Then, a knight stepped out of the crowd and everyone gathered round to look. He was dressed from head to toe in silver shining armour with a helmet on his head, so that only his face was showing. In his hands, he held a wooden sword. Alice noticed that the armour looked a bit too big and clunky for his actual body, which was quite small; it made a rattling noise whenever he moved, and he actually looked quite nervous about the fact that there was a sword in his hand, as though he had never held one before. But then, Alice knew, he wasn't a real knight, just an actor pretending to be one for the play.

'My name is St George,' he said in a voice that sounded more confident than he looked, 'and I have been sent on a mighty quest to save the beautiful Princess Margaret from the evil clutches of the Snap Dragon.'

He held his sword out in front of him and lunged forward, but as he did, he tripped over his own feet and stumbled. The crowd teetered with laughter. Alice had to giggle. A real knight wouldn't have tripped over his own feet.

Then, Princess Margaret stepped out of the crowd. She had long, wavy hair and wore a pink dress that flowed all the way down to the floor. She looked very fancy, so fancy that Alice almost believed that she was a real princess, though she knew that she wasn't, just an actress pretending to be one for the play.

'I have been kidnapped and kept prisoner here in the Snap Dragon's cave for three days now,' she said. 'I do hope someone will save me.'

'Fear not, sweet maiden,' bellowed St George proudly, 'I will save you.' He tripped again and dropped his sword.

The crowd all laughed and Alice giggled. He wasn't very good at pretending to be a hero.

Then, something incredible happened. Out of nowhere, the Snap Dragon suddenly appeared. He was just as Alice remembered: covered with scales of green and red, with some that glistened from yellow to gold. His belly was large and round and drooped so low that it almost touched the ground as he walked forwards. A bright flash of orange fire sparked from his open toothy jaws. The crowd all gasped in wonder and awe.

'It's the Snap Dragon,' they cried and began clapping and cheering and whistling with joy.

Alice knew that in the play the Snap Dragon was supposed to be the baddie, but she was so happy to see him that she couldn't help but clap and cheer too.

'No, no, no!' said St George to the crowd, quite angrily. 'You're not supposed to cheer, you're supposed to boo!' Alice could tell he wasn't too pleased that the Snap Dragon was stealing his limelight. 'Boo!' St George waved his hands about and tried to get the crowd to join in.

'Hooray!' they all cheered back. 'Hooray for the Snap Dragon!'

Annoyed, St George stepped towards the Snap Dragon and pretended to plunge the sword into his belly, though Alice could see the other side of the sword sticking out from behind his back and knew that the Snap Dragon wasn't really hurt at all.

'I have slain the Snap Dragon,' St George declared, sulkily. He walked towards Princess Margaret and took her by the hand.

'Sweet maiden, you are free.' Then the two of them began to dance. The crowd all clapped and cheered, then they began dancing too. They danced in a big procession down the street and the Snap Dragon led the way.

At the back of the crowd, even from on top of Peter's shoulders, Alice could hardly see the Snap Dragon any more through all the herds of moving people.

'Come on,' she called down to Peter. 'Let's see if we can get closer to the Snap Dragon.'

'We can't, Alice,' Peter said. 'We'll never push through all these people.'

Alice felt very disappointed. She had wanted to see the Snap Dragon so badly but knew there was no way she would ever get close to him now. She could just make out his head bobbing up and down amongst the swarms of people. For a split second, she caught sight of him catching sight of her, and she waved quickly.

Then, something extraordinary happened. Alice saw the Snap Dragon suddenly turn from the front of the procession and look straight towards her. Alice nearly fell off Peter's shoulders in surprise. The Snap Dragon was staring directly at her. Then, he started moving through the crowd towards her. People shuffled to one side and made room for him as he passed. He walked right up to Alice until he was so close to her and

Peter that she had to hold her breath to stop herself squealing with excitement.

Peter lifted Alice down from his shoulders. Alice reached out her hand and stroked the Snap Dragon's head. Then the Snap Dragon bent down his knees so that his body was lowered beside her.

'Go on, Alice,' said Peter. 'Climb on his back.'

Alice climbed up on the Snap Dragon's back. What happened next was too wonderful for words. As soon as Alice was sitting comfortably, the Snap Dragon began walking through the crowd and everybody clapped and cheered and reached out to shake her hand as she passed by them. It was the most magical thing that had ever happened to Alice. Even though it was a bit bumpy and she had to hold on tight, she really did feel as though she were flying.

After a while, the Snap Dragon gently sank to his knees so that she could slide off on to

the ground and then he made his way through the crowd again so that other children had a chance to see him.

Alice looked around her and saw that Mum, Peter, John and Matilda were close behind.

'Peter, Peter,' she ran up to her brother, 'Did you see it? Can you believe it? I rode on the back of a real live dragon!'

'Oh Alice,' Peter laughed and gave a fond smile. 'The Snap Dragon isn't a real dragon. It's a costume. There's a man inside pretending to be the Snap Dragon. An actor. Just like

St George and Princess Margaret are actors, the Snap Dragon is an actor too!'

Alice stared at Peter in disbelief. But of course the Snap Dragon was a real dragon. Peter was talking nonsense. She looked towards the Snap Dragon, who was dancing around amongst a hustle of gleeful children, and suddenly she began to notice things that she had never noticed before. The Snap Dragon only had two legs. A real dragon would have had four legs. She could see now that they were men's legs dressed in scaly leggings. And as for the Snap Dragon's body, Alice saw what she had never seen before, even when riding on his back: a man's head was poking out of a hole at the top.

Just like Peter had said, he was the man pretending to be the Snap Dragon. So, the Snap Dragon was a costume, and the man inside, an actor. Alice's eyes welled up. She wanted to cry but didn't. She could feel tears prickling as she stared at the Snap Dragon, but blinked through them because something else had caught her attention. She recognised the man's face. It was very strange; the more she stared, the more she recognised him. She knew who that man was. But, no, it couldn't be!

Alice's heart skipped a beat. She couldn't believe her eyes. The man inside the Snap Dragon wasn't an actor. The man was … Dad!

Yes, it really was Dad, but not in a way that she had ever seen him before. Dad was smiling and laughing and enjoying himself. She had never seen him look so happy as he danced and pranced about in the Snap Dragon costume. Her Dad, the very same Dad who never had time for her and never played with her, was the Snap Dragon. Only some moments ago, he had lifted her up on his back and they had paraded through crowds together and shared the most fantastic time.

Alice really did cry now. But not out of sadness. Out of happiness. Her Dad was the Snap Dragon and Alice was so, so happy.

Later on, when the Guild Day celebrations had ended, Alice and her family all went home together.

'I didn't know what the job today was going to be,' Dad explained to everyone. 'I just turned up because the man told me that I would get two shillings and sixpence for the day's work. That's a lot of money, so I couldn't refuse. Well, I had no idea that the day's job was to play the Snap Dragon at the Guild Day celebrations.'

He picked up Alice and swirled her around in his arms. 'It was the most fun I've ever had.'

All the family hugged each other and laughed. 'Oh, and the two shillings and sixpence,' added Dad, 'will be enough to buy us food for a week. We might even be able to afford something different to gruel.'

Alice didn't care about the silly old two shillings and sixpence. Her Dad was the Snap Dragon and she'd had the most amazing time playing with him all day.

After that, things changed around the house. Dad was still always busy; sometimes, he was even cross and worried too. He still didn't know where his next job was coming from and worked in many different jobs from day to day. But no matter what, Dad always found the time to play with Alice and the rest of the family. Alice forever remembered that magical Guild Day when Dad was the Snap Dragon and she had rode on his back through the crowd and everyone had clapped and cheered as they passed by. She remembered what a wonderful feeling it had been. Thanks to the Snap Dragon, Alice knew that even if Dad didn't always have the chance to show it, he loved her and the family more than anything else in the world.

It goes without saying, but still needs to be said: Alice and her family all lived happily ever after, in that very, very long time ago.

A MAMMOTH JOURNEY

Mammoth Skull

This story is set thousands and thousands of years ago when the world was full of animals.

Some of these animals are like the ones we see today: mice and hedgehogs and monkeys. But some of these animals have never been seen by the likes of you and me, such as the sabre-toothed cat. He wasn't much like a cat at all, at least not like the nice fluffy pet cats you might have at home who curl up on your lap and play with wool. He was the most vicious-looking cat you ever did see. He was called the sabre-toothed cat because of the two enormous and very sharp curved teeth he had at the front of his mouth. He was known throughout the land for his nasty temper and liked nothing better than to prowl the earth looking for trouble.

But the sabre-toothed cat wasn't the only big, ferocious animal around. There were lions and rhinos and big fearsome bears, but by far the biggest of all these creatures, the mightiest and most revered, was the steppe mammoth. If you want to know how big a steppe mammoth was, imagine an elephant. Now, imagine that the elephant is much, much bigger. The steppe mammoth was absolutely gigantic! So big, that if you stood on the ground and looked up at him, you would hardly be able see his head, he would be so high up above you. The mammoth looked a bit like an elephant too. He had four legs with big, heavy feet on which he clumped and stumped across the land, a long, long trunk which he could swish and swoosh about in the air and, on either side of his trunk, two enormous tusks which he could swing and slash all around him.

None of the dangerous animals dared to mess with the mammoth. Even the sabre-toothed cat would have run to the hills if he saw the mammoth was coming.

Luckily for the nicer animals, mammoths were herbivores. They ate herbs and leaves and shrubs which grew in the land around them.

The mammoth in this story was a herbivore too but even so, he never would have eaten another animal because he was quite a friendly creature. His favourite food was leaves.

Mammoths didn't really have names back then, but for the purpose of this story we'll call him Humphrey because it seems like a mammothy sort of name.

It was a warm summer's morning and Humphrey the mammoth was munching on some leaves from a tree. But they weren't very tasty leaves. In fact, they had no flavour at all.

'I don't think much of these leaves,' said Humphrey to himself. 'It must be because it's so warm in these parts, the sun has dried out the leaves and all the flavour has gone. I shall go on a journey to the North where the sky is wetter and the leaves are tastier. It should only take me till the end of the day, if I walk quickly.'

Now, this was a funny thing to say because mammoths weren't very good at walking quickly. They were so big and so heavy-footed that they could only walk very slowly.

Nonetheless, Humphrey put his best foot forward and began to make his way North.

He hadn't got very far, barely three steps forward even, when suddenly, from somewhere far, far below him, he heard a tiny voice. It was the teeniest, tiniest, squeakiest little voice you ever did hear.

'Excuse me, excuse me please,' said the tiny voice.

Humphrey looked down to see where the voice was coming from. Now remember, mammoths were so big that their feet were a long way down from their heads, so it took him a while to spot who was talking to him.

At last, he caught sight of a creature, no bigger than a pebble, sitting on a rock far, far below him. It was a little mouse. The mouse was all furry and brown with a quivering teeny black nose, pointy ears and whiskers. She stared up at Humphrey with her beady black eyes. Imagine how small she must have felt; a tiny thing staring up at great big enormous Humphrey! She looked a little afraid too because her body was shaking all over.

The mouse cleared her throat, 'Ahem', and said, 'Pardon me Sir, my name is Molly, Molly the mouse and how do you do? I couldn't help but overhear that you are travelling to the North. I was wondering if I may possibly accompany you on your journey. You see, I have heard tell that the sabre-toothed cat is travelling to these parts and will be here in no less than a day. I'm very frightened of the sabre-toothed cat. He eats little mice like me for breakfast.' She looked down at her teeny tiny mousy feet. 'I could ride on your back if that wouldn't be too much trouble?'

Humphrey listened attentively to what Molly had to say, but in spite of himself couldn't help but laugh, not because he was being mean, but because he wasn't scared of the sabre-toothed cat at all. Still, Humphrey didn't like to see animals that were so much smaller and more helpless than himself living in fear of the sabre-toothed cat. He smiled kindly down at Molly.

'But of course you may ride on my back, little Molly,' he said. 'It's no trouble at all, climb up my trunk and on to my back.'

Humphrey swung his enormous trunk down to the ground for Molly to climb up.

'Oh, thank you,' said Molly, and faster than a flash of light, she ran up Humphrey's trunk and nestled on to the skin of his gigantic back.

'We should be North by the end of the day,' Humphrey said. 'And if that sabre-toothed cat tries to stop us, well, I'd just like to see him try,' he chuckled to himself again. 'Right, off we go!'

He was about to lift up his trunk when all of a sudden Molly cried out, 'Wait! We can't go without my husband and eight children!'

And she called out, 'Husband! Eight children! Come along!'

And before Humphrey knew what was going on, nine other little mice had scurried out from behind the rock and, all at once, dashed up his trunk and on to his gigantic back.

Humphrey hadn't been expecting this, but still, he didn't mind in the least. He was so big and so strong that ten mice on his back made no difference whatsoever. In fact, the whole group felt no heavier than a feather. And so, off headed Humphrey with ten mice on his back, up to the North where the sky was wetter and the leaves were tastier.

At least, he tried to. No sooner had Humphrey started to walk than he suddenly felt something very sharp and prickly rub against his left front leg. The thing was so prickly, it felt as though a pine cone was digging into his skin.

'Ouch!' cried Humphrey. 'What is that very sharp and prickly thing?' He looked down at his foot.

'Pardon me, Sir,' said a muffled little voice from far, far below him, 'but it's me!'

Humphrey darted his eyes across the ground until at last he saw a creature burrowed in a clump of grass.

It was a little hedgehog. The hedgehog was a round, ball-shaped thing with a brown furry face and prickles all over.

'Hello,' said the hedgehog, 'my name is Harry. Harry the hedgehog and how do you do? I hope you don't mind my jeopardising your journey, only I've just heard tell that the sabre-toothed cat is travelling to these parts. I'm very scared of the sabre-toothed cat. He makes play things out of little hedgehogs like me. He'd pick off all my prickles and roll me around just for fun. Now, I've heard tell that you are travelling North and well, it's not that I would ask normally, only I've also heard tell that you are taking a family of mice with you ...'

'Wow,' said Humphrey, raising his eyes, 'news sure travels fast in this neck of the woods.'

'Well yes,' said Harry, 'even the trees have ears round here!' He looked down at his tiny feet and his small brown face blushed to the colour of beetroot. 'I was wondering, since you are taking the mice, perhaps you could take me too? If that wouldn't be too much trouble?'

'But of course,' cried Humphrey. 'It's no trouble at all. That sabre-toothed cat doesn't scare me one bit and I hate to see how much he scares you. You climb up on my back my prickly friend; you'll be safe as can be with me. We should be North by the end of the day and well away from that nasty sabre-toothed fellow.'

Humphrey swung down his enormous trunk for Harry to climb up. Harry curled himself into a prickly ball and rolled his way up Humphrey's trunk on to his gigantic back.

'Your prickles tickle!' laughed Humphrey.

When Harry was safely on his back, Humphrey was about to lift up his trunk when all of a sudden, Harry cried out 'Wait! We can't go without my wife and six children,' and he called out, 'Wife! Six children! Come along!'

And before Humphrey knew what was going on, seven hedgehogs popped up their prickly heads from out of the grass and, like Harry, they curled themselves into little balls and one by one, rolled up his trunk and on to his gigantic back.

Humphrey hadn't been expecting this. Still, he was so big and so strong that the whole group didn't make that much of a difference.

And so, off headed Humphrey with ten mice and eight hedgehogs on his back, up to the North where the sky was wetter and the leaves were tastier.

They hadn't got very far before Humphrey felt something slithery wrap around his back right leg. The slithery thing was very strong, like a tight coil of rope, and stopped him from moving forward any further.

He glanced down and had to tilt his head right back to see his legs behind him.

'What is that slithery thing wrapped around my back right leg?' Humphrey asked.

'Pardon me, Sir,' came a soft, low, hissy voice, 'but it's me.'

From the corner of his eye, Humphrey could just make out a grass snake. The grass snake was very well camouflaged on the ground because it was small and green like a blade of grass. But Humphrey could still see its alert little eyes and flickering forked tongue.

Now, Humphrey was a bit nervous around grass snakes. Even though they were small, they had an alarming habit of popping up out of nowhere and taking him by surprise. There was something very unpredictable about the way they could move, so fast, slippery and silent, so he always felt slightly on edge when he was around them.

'I can't see you properly if you're hiding back there, you snake in the grass,' Humphrey said. 'Come to my front so I can face you, mammoth to snake.'

In no time at all, the grass snake had popped out of the grass in front of him. Humphrey was unsettled by the speed at which the snake had slithered from his back to his front.

'Hello,' the grass snake said. 'My name is Gracie, Gracie the grass snake and how do you do? I hope you don't mind my sabotaging your stroll but I've heard tell that the sabre-toothed cat is travelling to these parts.'

'Yes,' said Humphrey, 'I think I know where this conversation is going. I suppose you want a ride on my back up to the North.'

'I don't like the sabre-toothed cat,' said Gracie, and her slithery body, which had been so still and serene, began suddenly shaking in panic. 'He'd tie my head to my tail and whirl me round his head like a lasso, wrap me round a tree and use me as a catapult ...'

'Alright, alright,' Humphrey interrupted her. 'I get the picture. Now, you grass snakes may well make me nervous but you've never done me any harm. I'll let you on my back but you must promise faithfully not to frighten the mice and hedgehogs.'

'Oh I promise, I promise!' said Gracie.

Humphrey swung down his enormous trunk and allowed Gracie to slither up on to his back. He was about to lift up his trunk when all of a sudden, Gracie cried, 'Wait! We can't leave without my husband and four children,' and she called out, 'Husband! Four children! Come along!'

Humphrey barely even had time to blink before five other grass snakes materialised without warning out of the grass. It was all he could do to narrow his eyes and watch them, as one by one they shot up his trunk and on to his gigantic back.

Humphrey hadn't been expecting this and he was beginning to feel the extra weight. Still, it wasn't that bad and so, off headed Humphrey with ten mice, eight hedgehogs and six grass snakes on his back, up to the North where the sky was wetter and the leaves were tastier.

They had travelled for quite some distance when they came upon a large clump of trees. Humphrey was very glad of the shade. He was beginning to get a little worn out with all those animals on his back.

'I'll just cool myself for a while under the branches of this nice tree,' he said. He hadn't cooled himself for long when, all of a sudden, there came a great rustling in the tree tops above him. Then, as if from nowhere, a creature swinging on a branch came crashing through the trees and straight towards Humphrey.

Humphrey didn't even have time to duck before the creature landed right at the top of his trunk and stared at him square in the eyes.

It was a macaque monkey. The monkey was small and covered in brown hair. He had a little round furry face and a mischievous twinkle in his eyes.

'Hello!' he said. 'My name is Marcus. Marcus the macaque monkey and how do you do? I hope you don't mind my ambushing your amble but

I have heard tell that the sabre-toothed cat is travelling to these parts. You know he makes mincemeat out of monkeys like me?'

Humphrey sighed. 'It seems the sabre-toothed cat is bad news for everyone. Listen Marcus, there's no need to say any more. In fact, don't say anything at all. Once you monkeys start talking you never stop. The answer to the question you were about to ask is yes, you may ride on my back to the North and whilst you're at it, bring your wife and kids. But only, and I repeat only, if you promise to behave yourself and not be disruptive. You monkeys are nothing but mischief but whilst you're on my back you play by my rules and make no trouble and stay quiet!'

Marcus clamped his hand over his mouth and nodded sincerely.

'Oh,' he whispered through his hand, 'may I call out to my wife and two kids?'

'Go for it,' said Humphrey.

Marcus called out, 'Wife! Two kids! Come along!' and in no time at all, four macaque monkeys were sitting on Humphrey's gigantic back. The group were all really starting to feel quite heavy now. Humphrey was very grateful for his strong, sturdy muscles which he now had to put to good use, especially as the monkeys had already started messing about, rocking from side to side and rolling over each other.

'Excuse me,' Humphrey coughed sternly, 'my back is not a playground! Behave yourselves!'

And with that, off headed Humphrey with ten mice, eight hedgehogs, six grass snakes and four macaque monkeys on his back, up to the North where the sky was wetter and the leaves were tastier.

They had been travelling for some time when they came across two spotted hyaenas. The hyaenas looked like dogs, only bigger, and their fur was covered with big black spots. The two were playing together on a patch of dry land. Humphrey wasn't a huge fan of hyaenas. They were usually very troublesome creatures, far more so than monkeys. Monkeys were playful but hyaenas were a pain because they never stopped laughing.

Humphrey hoped he could walk past without them noticing but this was wishful thinking.

As soon as the hyaenas clapped eyes on Humphrey they burst into wild, howling shrieks of laughter.

'What *do* you look like?' one of them cackled, rolling around on the floor, clutching his sides. 'I've never seen anything so funny in all my life!'

'Yeah,' piped up the other, 'you look ridiculous with all those animals on your back. What are you, a walking safari?'

Humphrey held his head high. He resisted the urge to tell them how rude they were and strode on without a word.

'You look stupid,' the hyaenas sang after him.

Suddenly, Marcus the macaque monkey clambered on to Humphrey's head and addressed the hyaenas.

'Oh yeah?' he said. 'Stupid, you say? Well, the laugh's on you mate!'

'No!' said Humphrey through gritted teeth. 'Don't tell them, don't tell them!'

But Marcus kept talking. 'We're travelling North because the sabre-toothed cat is coming to these parts. He'll be here by the end of the day,' he said.

As soon as he said the words 'sabre-toothed cat' the hyaenas stopped laughing and rolling about on the floor. They sat up and stood still, staring at Marcus through eyes wide with terror.

'We're hitching a ride on Humphrey's back,' Marcus continued proudly, 'but I suppose you'll just have to stay here and get eaten.'

'No!' cried the hyaenas and they began scurrying about and falling over each other in a blind panic. 'Not the sabre-toothed cat, we'll never outrun him, help us! Help, help!'

'Oh, I would help,' said Humphrey 'but you will be too heavy for me and besides, you hyaenas are nothing but trouble.'

'Oh please,' the hyaenas began to yelp and wail. 'Please! Please! We're not trouble, we're Sally and

Sammy the spotted hyaenas and we'll be very good, we promise, please take us with you!'

Now, Humphrey might not have particularly liked hyaenas but he didn't feel comfortable seeing them so distraught. 'Oh alright,' he said. 'I'll do my best to carry you all.'

Humphrey bent his knees and slowly lowered himself down to the ground. He had to be very careful not to accidentally drop any of the other animals on his back. Sally and Sammy, the two very relieved spotted hyaenas, clambered on to his gigantic back. Some of the smaller animals were a bit disgruntled by their presence, but they knew that the hyaenas could do them no harm because Humphrey would never have allowed it.

As soon as they were settled on Humphrey's back, the hyaenas stopped wailing and looking terrified and started to laugh again.

'Ha ha,' they laughed. 'That sabre-toothed cat is going to be so disappointed when he gets here and finds there's nothing to eat.'

'Yes,' grunted Humphrey, 'well he'd better be coming after all this.' And with that, off headed Humphrey with ten mice, eight hedgehogs, six grass snakes, four macaque monkeys and two spotted hyaenas on his back, up to the North where the sky was wetter and the leaves were tastier.

Presently, they came upon a pool of water where a deer was taking a drink. The deer was tall with sleek brown fur and she carried herself gracefully on her four long legs. Humphrey liked deer. He thought they were beautiful, elegant creatures.

He nodded to the deer and was about to walk on, when suddenly he realised that he recognised her. It was Dolores, Dolores the deer. The two often bumped into each other whilst on their separate journeys and she was always so friendly and polite.

Now, Humphrey was really very tired and worn out what with carrying all those heavy animals on his back; he felt he couldn't possibly carry one more, but the thought of leaving Dolores on her own when the sabre-toothed cat was on foot made his heart sink. She wouldn't stand a chance against that beastly cat. He decided that for Dolores, he could make the exception.

'Dolores,' he called out to her. Dolores looked up and smiled as soon as she saw him, though her large, brown, soulful eyes quickly turned quizzical when she saw the animals on his back.

'Not much time to explain,' Humphrey said. 'Listen Dolores, the sabre-toothed cat is travelling to these parts and I'm helping this lot get to the North where they'll be safe. I don't want to leave you behind. Climb on my back and I'll take you.'

He lowered himself carefully to the ground. Dolores didn't argue but climbed straight on his back. She trusted Humphrey.

'Thank you, Humphrey,' she said. 'What would we all do without you?'

And so, off headed Humphrey with ten mice, eight hedgehogs, six grass snakes, four macaque monkeys, two spotted hyaenas and a deer on his back, up to the North where the sky was wetter and the leaves were tastier.

Humphrey walked for many miles. His bones ached and he could feel his muscles growing weaker and weaker from all the strain, but still he pressed on.

By the time they had nearly reached the North, he was hot and sweating.

After a while, they came across a big brown bear sitting on the ground all alone. The bear's head was drooping down and he looked very sad and sorry for himself.

The animals were all frightened of the big brown bear. 'Keep walking Humphrey,' they called. 'Keep walking!'

But Humphrey did not keep walking. Instead he stopped and stared at the big brown bear. Bears were usually very proud creatures. They walked the earth upright and unafraid. Humphrey didn't like to see one so down in the dumps.

Then he noticed that the bear was cradling a wounded leg. The bear looked up at Humphrey with big, sorrowful eyes. 'Oh,' he said in a miserable voice, 'Hello. My name is Ben, Ben the brown bear. You must be Humphrey. I've heard all about you. You're travelling to the North, away from the sabre-toothed cat. I wasn't afraid of him; I could take him in a fight if I had to, that is until I wounded my leg. I'll never get away from him now if he tries to catch me …' he trailed off and suddenly looked hopeful. 'I don't suppose …'

'Say no more,' Humphrey said. He lowered himself to the ground for Ben to climb on to his gigantic back.

'No!' cried the animals. 'That big brown bear can look after himself!'

'He's wounded his leg,' said Humphrey. 'He needs help just like the rest of you.'

And with that, off headed Humphrey with ten mice, eight hedgehogs, six grass snakes, four macaque monkeys, two spotted hyaenas, one deer and one big brown bear on his back, up to the North where the sky was wetter and the leaves were tastier.

Humphrey walked and walked and walked. His back grew weaker and weaker and weaker. He heaved and hoed and pushed and toed, onwards and onwards until he could hardly feel his feet any more. Beads of sweat ran down his forehead and his eyes grew blurry. After some time, he grew faint and began to see black dots in the air.

Then, all of a sudden, Marcus the macaque monkey cried out, 'We're here! We're North. The air is different and the land and trees are different too. We're safe and far away from that smelly old sabre-toothed cat.'

'Hooray!' the animals all cheered. 'Let us down, Humphrey!'

Humphrey tried to lower himself steadily but our poor mammoth was so utterly exhausted that his knees gave way and he collapsed to the ground with an enormous, great thud. The animals were so excited, they didn't notice what a terrible and tired state Humphrey was in. They all scurried off in different directions to find their nearest natural habitat. The mice, hedgehogs and grass snakes scuttled into the grass, the macaque monkeys headed straight for the trees, the deer went to find the nearest pool of water and the spotted hyaenas helped the wounded big brown bear to walk to a fresh patch of land. Humphrey was left lying on the ground, alone.

Well, not quite alone.

Molly the mouse was sitting beside him. 'That was a very brave thing you did, Humphrey,' she said, 'and kind and considerate and courageous. You put the needs of all us animals in front of your own. Thank you. I will never forget what you did for us, Humphrey. Acts of bravery and kindness, like yours, should never be forgotten.'

'Oh,' Humphrey smiled at her sleepily. 'Thank you, Molly. I'm so happy you're all safe now that we're finally here, although ...' he looked confused, 'I can't seem to remember why I was coming in the first place.'

'I remember!' said Molly, 'Wait there!' She raced off and seconds later reappeared with an armful of leaves. She placed them down near Humphrey's mouth.

'Oh, that's right!' said Humphrey. He nibbled at the leaves. 'Excellent, they really are much tastier. Thank you for bringing them, Molly.' Humphrey sighed and leaned back his head. 'That was a very long journey,' he said. 'I think I'll stay lying down here for a while and have a rest.'

'Yes,' said Molly. 'You have a nice rest, Humphrey. You've earned it. I'll watch over you.'

Humphrey closed his eyes.

This seems like a good place to end the story, but Humphrey's long journey isn't quite finished. The story continues thousands and thousands of years later. Not too long ago, a group of people found some fossils on a beach. Fossils are old animal bones or impressions of plants embedded in rock, but these particular fossils didn't belong to *any* old animal. They belonged to Humphrey and were found exactly on the patch of land where he was lying down for his rest.

Today, that patch of land is called West Runton and Humphrey is famously known as the West Runton Mammoth. At Norfolk Collections Centre you can see his skull and one of his enormous tusks, which is being preserved for all time and on display for everyone to see. In this way, the memory of Humphrey lives on forever.

As Molly the mouse would tell you, acts of bravery and kindness, like Humphrey's, should never be forgotten.

THE BOY WHO SAVED MUSTARD FROM TASTING LIKE SMELLY FEET

Mustard Stamper

Ask anyone living in Norwich today who is one of the city's most famous historical figures and many will tell you Jeremiah Colman. The reason Jeremiah Colman is such a famous historical figure is because he made Colman's Mustard. This was a whole 200 years ago but I bet you've heard of Colman's Mustard! You might have had it on your hot dog, in a burger or with your egg and chips! Jeremiah Colman was the first person in his family to make the mustard and all these years later Colman's Mustard is still being made. The people of Norwich love their Colman's Mustard!

But this story isn't really about Jeremiah Colman. This story is about someone who helped Jeremiah Colman to become as famous as he is today. That someone was a boy, whose name was, well, Boy.

You see, unlike Jeremiah Colman, Boy isn't a famous historical figure at all. In fact, it's fair to say that he is the opposite of famous because no one has heard of him, though you certainly will have heard of him by the end of this story.

Boy was an orphan, which means he didn't have any parents so there was no one to tell him, or anyone else for that matter, who he was. There were lots of other things Boy didn't have, besides parents. He didn't have any family or relations, no grandparents or cousins, no Uncle Matthew to play football with or Auntie Mabel to give him sloppy wet kisses. Another thing Boy didn't have was a home. Instead, he lived on the streets, which wasn't much fun. The streets were rough and dirty, and with no roof over his head, when it rained, well, Boy got wet. You see, back in those days, if you didn't have a family or home no one looked after you or helped you at all so you would have been left to fend for yourself – just like Boy.

Another thing Boy didn't have, a very tricky thing to be without, was money. Without money, he couldn't buy food and he didn't much like the thought of stealing food from other people because he knew that was wrong, so most of the time Boy had a very rumbly stomach.

This may seem like a sad picture we've painted for Boy, but surprisingly, he didn't really mind not having any of these because there were lots of things that Boy *did* have. He did have friends; there was Jenny and Tommy and Jake – orphans just like him – who lived on the streets, and they all helped each other out.

He did have clothes and boots which had been made for him by a kind shopkeeper who saw him in the street one day and took pity. She had made him such an enormous coat that when it rained, Jenny and Tommy and Jake could all huddle underneath it like an umbrella.

He did have, and this was a very useful thing to have, acrobatic skills. He could somersault, cartwheel, backflip, stand on his head till he was blue in the face and juggle with rotten fruit that had gone so bad even hungry Boy couldn't eat it. People would gather round to watch and clap and toss him coins, so Boy could buy food for himself and his friends.

The only thing Boy did mind not having, the thing he really, really wanted, was a name. A name wasn't something Boy could just make in the way he could make friends and a home and money. You see, Boy believed that a name was a very special sort of thing that someone else had to make for you. That is to say, in order for him to have a real name, a proper name, someone else had to give him a name, the way that parents give their children names. But since Boy didn't have any parents, it seemed very unlikely that this would ever happen. Everyone on the streets just called him 'Boy.'

Now, one day, Boy was scavenging the street for food because he had run out of the pennies he had earned from standing on his head. He was down on his hands and knees, fumbling in a dirty old gutter.

'What are you doing, boy?' A voice came out of nowhere. Boy looked up slowly to see that a man was standing above him. The man was tall and dressed in fine clothes so that Boy could tell that he was quite well-to-do. He had a handsome, kindly face and a twinkle in his eye.

'Well,' asked the man, 'what are you doing?'

'Oh,' said Boy, 'I'm er, scavenging for food, if it' s no trouble to you, Sir.'

'Well, it's no trouble to me,' said the man, 'but you might find your tummy is in trouble if you eat food from down there. It's filthy, all that dirt is not very good for you.'

'I don't worry about dirt when I'm hungry, Sir,' said Boy.

'Well, you should,' said the man. 'Here, take this,' and he held out his hand to Boy.

Boy stood up nervously, unsure of what the man was going to give him. He held out his hand and the next thing he knew, the man had slipped a shiny silver coin into his palm. Boy stared at the coin in disbelief. Usually, he had to juggle or backflip or at least stand on his head till he was blue in the face in order for people to give him money. But this man had simply handed him money and Boy hadn't even had to do anything!

'Go and buy yourself some proper food from the bakery,' the man said. 'That should be enough to see you through the week.'

'Why, thank you, Sir!' said Boy. 'Very generous! Much obliged!'

He was about to dart off to the bakery straight away when the man said, 'Before you go, tell me, what is your name, boy?'

'Boy,' said Boy.

The man raised an eyebrow. 'Very funny,' he said.

Boy shrugged. 'Nothing funny about it, Sir. That's my name.'

'Well, my name,' said the man, 'is Jeremiah Colman.'

'Oh,' said Boy, then after a pause, because he didn't know what else to say, he blurted, 'never heard of you.'

Jeremiah Colman chuckled. 'Well Boy, I like that you are honest. No, I wouldn't expect you to have heard of me. No one has heard of me, though one day I very much hope that everyone will know my name.'

'Oh?' said Boy. 'Why's that Mr Colman Sir?'

'Well,' Jeremiah Colman explained, 'it's like this. I've started making my very own brand of mustard. It's called "Colman's Mustard" – after me! I have a factory in a place called Stoke Holy Cross where I work exceptionally hard to make this Colman's Mustard. It's very important to me that the mustard tastes excellent because I want people to enjoy eating it as much as I enjoy making it. The only trouble is, I've only just started out and because no one knows who I am, it's very difficult to find someone who is willing to test the mustard for me to see whether or not it is of the impeccable standard that I want it to be. What I need is an honest opinion from someone who is not afraid to speak their mind and that someone, Boy, is you.'

'I can speak my mind right enough,' said Boy. 'Where's the mustard? I'll test it for you.'

'Ah, well,' said Jeremiah, 'I don't want you just to test it, Boy. I want you to go out and test my mustard on the public and by that I mean the ordinary working folk of Norwich. You see, the reason I've travelled from my factory in Stoke Holy Cross to Norwich today is because I know the city is full of honest, hard-working people, the sort of people I want to enjoy my mustard. Here's how it works: I give you a sample of my mustard and you go out and ask several people to taste it and tell you what they think. No one's really heard of Colman's Mustard but nonetheless, don't mention my name – I don't want to get a bad reputation if people don't like it. Just tell them that it's ordinary mustard. Then, you report back to me with what they said. That way, I'll know what people really think about my mustard and how I can improve it.'

He tapped his nose and winked at Boy, 'A secret operation.'

Boy's head was buzzing with the brilliance of the task at hand. He'd never been in charge of a secret operation before.

Jeremiah Colman reached into the pocket of his black coat and produced a small wooden bowl. Boy peered inside the bowl and saw a good deal of bright yellow mustard powder, along with a little wooden spoon. Then Jeremiah Colman took out a little jug of water with a stopper.

'Mix a drop of water with a bit of powder to make the mustard paste,' he explained. 'Now, let's agree to report back to each other, at this spot tomorrow morning.'

'Right you are, Sir,' said Boy. Jeremiah walked off and Boy ran into the busy streets of Norwich.

The streets were very crowded indeed. There were lots of people about. It wasn't long before Boy had bumped into a man who was wheeling a large cart full of barrels. The man looked hot, sweaty and bothered.

'Excuse me, Sir,' Boy chirruped at the man as he scooted past with his big cart of barrels. 'Would you like to try some of this mustard?'

'Eh?' said the man, turning his sweaty, beetroot face towards Boy. He looked very agitated.

'Mustard,' said Boy, pointing at the wooden bowl in his hand as though spelling it out for the man. 'What folk put on their food.'

The man gave Boy such a look as if to say he didn't have time for this nonsense and bustled on by with his cart. Boy was not one to give up so quickly. He ran after the man and jumped in front of him so that he could go no further, forcing him to stop abruptly.

'You look tired, Sir. Why not stop for a rest and try some of this mustard?'

The man looked even more agitated. 'If it will get you to shut up and go away then alright.'

Boy mixed a drop of water into his little wooden bowl of powder and handed the man a sample of the mustard on the spoon. The man put the spoon to his mouth.

'Well?' asked Boy. 'What do you think?'

The man shrugged, as though he couldn't really taste anything at all.

Then, all of a sudden, his beetroot-red face turned white as a sheet. He opened his mouth and spat out the mustard on to the floor! Boy jumped back in surprise.

Then, to his amazement, the man punched one of the barrels on his cart, making a large gaping hole out of which flooded a gush of water. The man bent backwards so that he was standing directly beneath the gush of water, opening his mouth wide to let the water flow in.

'That bad, eh?' said Boy, watching the man in bewilderment.

The man was busy gurgling with the water. At last, he gulped down one great big mouthful, turned to Boy and with a look of disgust said, 'Feet. Pongy old whiffy old smelly old feet.'

'You mean this mustard tastes like feet?' Boy exclaimed.

But the man had clearly had enough chit-chat for that day. He grabbed the handles of his cart and with a grunt, walked on.

Boy continued on his quest. It wasn't long before he bumped into a woman who was walking with a cow on a rope.

'Excuse me Mrs,' said Boy, 'would you like to try some of this mustard?'

The woman sniffed. 'Yeah, why not?'

Boy handed her the spoon with the mustard. No sooner had she put it to her lips than she spat it back out again. 'Puh! Pongy feet! Don't bother making any more of that,' and she continued abruptly on her way.

Boy tried several more people that day, but every one of them had the same reaction!

Whiffy feet! Yucky feet! Pongy old pooey old feet! Really, really smelly feet!

At last, exhausted, Boy took a break and went to the bakery to buy some bread with the coin Jeremiah had given him. Walking back through the streets with a loaf in his hands, he spotted his friend, Jenny, sitting on the curb of the pavement. Jenny was a flower seller; she picked wild flowers that she could sell to passers-by, though by the looks of things, it didn't seem as if she'd had a very good day. Her basket was still full of wild pink and purple flowers, which meant she hadn't sold many and poor Jenny looked very dejected.

'Alright Jenny?' chirped Boy. He halved the loaf of bread he was carrying. 'Here, get your teeth round this.'

Jenny's eyes widened with delight as she saw the food. 'Oh, thank you Boy!' she said, and taking the half of loaf that he handed her, she crammed her mouth around a piece in seconds flat.

'Here,' said Boy, 'do you want to try a bit of this mustard?' He scraped a tiny portion of the mustard over the rest of Jenny's bread.

'Urgh, Boy!' cried Jenny as soon as she tried it. 'It tastes like smelly feet. Why would you make me eat that?'

Boy giggled. 'Sorry Jenny. Just wanted to check you'd have the same reaction as everyone else. I'm testing this mustard for a friend you see, his name is Jeremiah Colman and he's a very nice person. He wants to be well known for his mustard and asked me to test it by getting people to try it and telling me what they think, but I'm afraid everyone says it tastes of smelly feet. I feel really bad for Mister Colman, Jenny. He was very kind to me, I don't just want to say "sorry Mister Colman Sir, your mustard tastes like smelly feet and goodbye" but at the same time, I promised I would give him an honest opinion. If only there was some way that I could still be honest with him but at the same time do something that would actually help. But I don't know anything about mustard!'

'You could start by telling the mustard stampers to wash their feet,' said Jenny.

'Eh?' Boy looked at her confused, as though he couldn't believe the words that had just come out of her mouth. 'What you on about Jenny?'

'Well,' Jenny said, 'mustard is made from mustard seeds. In the process of changing the mustard seeds to a liquid, the seeds have to be crushed right down to form a powdery substance.'

'Eh?' Boy looked at Jenny startled. 'I had no idea you knew that!'

'Sometimes,' Jenny continued, 'people crush the mustard seeds by stamping them with their hands or, in some cases, their feet.'

Boy blinked at Jenny, utterly amazed as she continued.

'And since this foot-stamping business is not entirely uncommon, I wouldn't be surprised if that's the reason why your friend's mustard stinks to the high heavens of filthy old feet.'

Boy laughed. 'Jenny, how do you know all this?'

Jenny shrugged. 'I know stuff and things,' she said. 'Ain't stupid.'

'You're certainly not,' said Boy. 'You're much smarter than I am! It strikes me that what Mister Colman needs is some sort of mustard-stamping device; something that can crush the mustard seeds just as fast, quickly and cheaply, but will save his mustard from tasting like smelly feet … wait a minute,' and his eyes flashed with excitement, 'I can help Mister Colman. I just have to invent something.'

At that moment, Boy's friends Tommy and Jake showed up. Between the two of them, they were carrying a large wooden object.

'It's an old closet,' called Tommy. 'Someone threw it out and there's a whole pile of old wooden furniture back down the road. We figured we could use it for firewood. What do you say folks? Nice big bonfire?'

Boy sprang to his feet. 'Oh no you don't!' he cried. 'That's not firewood. That's a mustard stamper!'

'What?' Jenny, Tommy and Jake all stared at Boy, baffled.

'Just you wait,' said Boy. 'I've got a brilliant idea.'

He led the group to the local friendly blacksmith where they borrowed some tools. All night long, Boy chopped and chiselled and hammered away. Everyone chipped in to help. By the end of the night, the finished result looked something like this!

Boy explained to his group of friends: 'The mustard stamper works like this – bang the wooden levers up and down to stamp the mustard seeds in the tray below!'

The next day, Boy decided to leave his creation in the spot where he and Jeremiah Colman had agreed to meet. He didn't have the heart to tell Jeremiah Colman to his face that his mustard tasted like smelly feet, so he left a note.

Boy didn't know how to write, but he asked the kind shopkeeper who made his coat if she would write it for him:

> Mr Colman Sir, here is my honest opinion along with a proposed solution. Smelly feet don't go down a treat. Try this to give your mustard a fresh twist.

Some days later, Boy was scavenging for food beneath a dirty old gutter.

'What are you doing, Boy?' came a voice from nowhere.

Boy looked up. 'Mister Colman, Sir!' and he jumped to his feet.

Jeremiah Colman beamed an enormous smile. 'I came to thank you, Boy,' he said. 'That mustard-stamping device you made me is most excellent. So excellent, I've replicated the item, improved it to a high standard and produced quite a few for my factory. They do a fantastic job of crushing the mustard seeds. No more smelly feet!'

'That's wonderful,' said Boy.

'Yes, it is,' said Jeremiah Colman. 'But that isn't the end of it. I want to repay you for your help, Boy. As a thank you, I want you to come and work for me in my mustard factory in Stoke Holy Cross. You will be fairly paid for your work and the conditions are much nicer than here on the streets. In fact, my factory is well known for being a good and safe place to work. You will have a warm roof over your head and we have breakfast and dinner every day, so you'll never go hungry. What do you say?'

Boy was about to leap at the chance, when something made him stop. 'It's not that I don't appreciate the offer Mister Colman Sir,' he said. 'I'd love to come and work for you in your factory. But I'm afraid I can't leave my friends, Jenny and Tommy and Jake. They live on the streets too and we all look after each other, you see.'

'Oh, but they can come too,' said Jeremiah Colman. 'You can all come and work in my factory. You've helped me more than I can say. Is there anything else you want?'

Boy thought for a moment. He scratched his head. 'Well Sir, there is this one thing I've always wanted.'

'Yes Boy, what's that?'

Boy looked down at his feet. He felt a bit embarrassed about saying it, but this was the first time anyone had ever asked him what he wanted, so he knew that it was now or never. 'A name,' said Boy.

Jeremiah Colman looked startled for a moment. Then he broke out into laughter. 'But, Boy, if you wanted a name, why didn't you just give one to yourself?'

'I can't, Sir,' said Boy. 'You see, a name is a very special sort of thing, not the sort of thing I can just make in the way I can make other things like, well, friends or money or a mustard stamper. In order for a name to be a real name, a proper name, it has to be given to you by someone else.'

Jeremiah Colman stared at Boy in disbelief. 'You mean, all these years you've gone without a name, simply because no one would give you one?'

Boy nodded sheepishly. 'Is that stupid?' he asked.

'Oh no my dear Boy, it's not stupid,' said Jeremiah Colman. 'It's heartbreaking. I'll happily give you a name. I can think of a good one for you right now. Although, it feels like quite a responsibility, giving you a name to use for the rest of your life! Why don't I whisper it to you, then if you don't like it, shake your head and I'll give you another.'

Jeremiah Colman leant in very close to Boy's ear and whispered the name. As soon as Boy heard it, he smiled the biggest smile that he had ever smiled.

'Thank you Mister Colman Sir, I love it.'

After that, things were very different for everybody. Jenny, Tommy and Jake all worked in the Mustard Factory at Stoke Holy Cross. They never went cold or hungry again. Jenny was especially glad that she didn't have to sell flowers any more.

Jeremiah Colman made more mustard stampers to use in his factories and continued to make Colman's Mustard. The mustard was a great success. Soon everybody had heard of Colman's Mustard and just as Jeremiah Colman had hoped, everyone knew his name. Some years later, his great-nephew Jeremiah James Colman continued the family business and his mustard was so popular that even Queen Victoria ate it.

As for Boy, well, he was never seen or heard of again. Rumour has it he spent the rest of his life working happily at the Stoke Holy Cross works. But that boy answered to a different name, a real name, a proper name that had been given to him by none other than Jeremiah Colman. He was happy just to have a name; he didn't need it to be a famous one.

You see, a name isn't the sort of thing you can just make in the way that you can make other things like friends or a home or money or a mustard stamper – or a story.

OUR
SECRET HOME
St Gregory's Rood Screen

Many years ago, in a time called the Medieval age, the city of Norwich was a very important place to live. It was one of the busiest and most wealthy places in all of England and the people who lived there felt very lucky that this fine city was their home.

In this time, there lived a little kitten called Thomas. Thomas's fur was black as midnight and soft as snow. He had sharp pointy ears, a keen little nose and whiskers delicate as spiderwebs. His tail was a neat little wand which he could swish and swoosh from side to side.

Thomas didn't know much about the time he lived in. He didn't know it was called the 'Medieval age'; he didn't know that Norwich was a very important place to live; he didn't even know that the city was called Norwich.

It's fair to say that Thomas didn't really know much about anything. Most days, all Thomas ever knew was that he was cold and hungry and lonely. You see, Thomas was a street kitten. He didn't have a home or a family to look after him or feed him or love him. He wandered the streets day and night searching for food and company. Thomas dearly wanted someone to stroke him or play with him but he often found that nobody seemed to like him or even want to come near him, and he didn't know why.

One particularly cold, dreary and windy day it was raining hard and Thomas was desperately looking for somewhere to find shelter. He hated the rain; the way it pelted down in great big droplets made him nervous and he didn't like his fur to get wet. At last, Thomas stumbled on a building with an open door. The building was quite the biggest he had ever seen with a roof that slanted upwards towards the grey sky.

Inside the building, it wasn't much warmer than it was outside but still, he was grateful to be dry. For a moment, Thomas stood in the doorway and looked around to see that there were no people there. Whenever he sneaked inside a building, people usually shouted at him to 'get out!' But in here he was relieved to see that there was no one around. It was all very quiet and a sense of stillness hovered in the air. How very big it was! Looking up at the roof which was so high above him, Thomas had never felt so tiny. The room was a big empty space and at the end of the space he could see a large wooden panel which stretched from one side of the room to the other. In the middle of the panel was an arch-shaped doorway which seemed to lead on to a different part of the building. On each side of the doorway the panels were covered with lots of bright and colourful paintings. It was nice to see such a warm and decorative sight when the world outside was so gloomy and grey. Thomas walked up the middle of the big room to get a better look at the pictures.

When he got closer, there was one picture in particular which really caught his eye and he instinctively walked straight towards that one.

The background of the picture was blue with golden stars. A woman with a red dress stood holding a tower in her hands. She looked very elegant and majestic and there was a slight smile across her face as though she had a secret she wanted to tell you. It was lovely to see someone looking friendly for a change and Thomas wished that she could come to life out of the picture and play with him.

All of a sudden, Thomas heard footsteps coming from the other end of the room. He almost jumped out of his fur – what would someone do if they found him? Quick as a flash, Thomas darted through the arch-shaped door in the middle of the panel and hid on the other side. He heard the footsteps slowly growing louder and louder as they came closer and closer and he shuddered with fright. There was no door leading out of the building anywhere around him. Thomas was trapped hiding where he was with no escape from the person who was coming towards him.

'What's this?' a voice echoed across the room. 'Little paw prints across the floor?'

Thomas looked down at his feet. Oh no! He hadn't realised that they were covered in mud. He must have left muddy paw prints in a trail all over the floor. A trail leading right to him! Whoever it was would surely find him now.

'One, two, three, four …' The person was starting to count the paw prints. Not long now till they found him.

'Five, six, seven …' It was strange, thought Thomas, the person didn't sound particularly angry or cross. It was quite a nice voice, soft and warm. It sounded very much like the voice of a little girl.

'Eight, nine, ten …' The next thing Thomas knew, he was staring the person right in the face. Sure enough, it was a little girl. She was a small, pale thing with tangled streaks of red hair. She wore a plain brown dress that looked very dirty and Thomas also noticed that there was dirt all over her hands and face. She looked every bit as swept off the street as he was. But despite a somewhat tatty appearance, her eyes were wide and shining.

'Oh look at you!' she cried and scooped Thomas up in her arms. 'You are just adorable!'

Thomas felt very confused. No one had ever been so affectionate with him before.

'But listen,' said the little girl. 'You're not supposed to be in this part of the church. This is the chancel, only the priest is allowed in here. If he had found you, or anyone else for that matter, you would have got very, very told off.'

She moved back on to the other side of the panel and sat down on the floor, placing Thomas carefully in her lap.

'Have you ever been inside a church before?'

Thomas shook his head.

'Well,' said the little girl, 'that explains why you don't know the rules. As I said, no one but the priest is allowed inside the chancel behind the panel. But we are allowed inside this part which is called the nave.'

Thomas nodded as if to say that he now understood. He was still completely baffled that she was being friendly and kind to him when nobody ever even wanted to go near him.

'Oh, but you're not even supposed to be here at all!' the little girl said. 'Nobody here likes cats. They think that cats are only good for catching rats and some people even think that cats are friends with witches and can do nasty magic spells.'

Thomas stared at her in disbelief. So that was why nobody ever played with him or even wanted to come near him! But he didn't know any witches or nasty magic spells. He didn't want to do harm to anyone. Thomas let out a little yelp of distress.

'Oh, don't worry,' said the little girl. 'I know that's not true. You couldn't possibly mean ill will towards anybody. Look at you, you're a little ball of fluff!' She tickled his tummy and Thomas rolled on his back and purred.

'Now listen and listen carefully,' the little girl became instructive all of a sudden, 'because I'm going to tell you about the church.'

Thomas was very glad that the little girl knew he was not friends with a witch. He curled up in her lap and listened attentively to her talking. It was nice to have someone explain things to him that he didn't know and she certainly seemed very eager to share her knowledge about the building.

'It's called Saint Gregory's Church,' said the little girl. 'I know the names of everything you see. The picture of the lady is part of what we call a rood screen. She is called Saint Barbara and as you see, that building she is holding is a tower.'

The little girl grinned. 'I expect you're wondering how I know all these things?'

Thomas nodded.

'I work here,' she said. 'I'm the sweeping girl, you see my broom in the corner there?' She pointed to a corner of the room and there was a little broom made from twigs propped up against the wall. 'You've made a secret home here, haven't you? Do you live out on the street you poor thing?'

Thomas nodded.

'I used to live on the street too,' said the little girl. 'I don't have a family or anything and I was homeless, that is until the church took me in and let me work for them. Why, I didn't even have a name until I was given one.' She gasped suddenly.

'Oh but how rude, I haven't even introduced myself! My name is Maude. What's your name?'

'Thomas,' said Thomas, although he knew she couldn't very well understand him. He had tried talking to humans before and they just didn't understand cats the way cats understood humans. All Maude would have heard was 'meow!'

Maude laughed. 'I can't very well call you *Meow* can I?'

Suddenly she jumped up on her feet and Thomas tumbled from her lap. 'Come on, let's play! I bet you can't run as fast as I can!' The next thing Thomas knew they were running round and round the church in a race. They played for ages and ages. Thomas had never felt so happy or excited. He loved Maude more than anything.

After an hour or so Maude said that lots of people would be coming to the church soon and it was time for her to sweep and get everything ready.

'Oh, and clear up these muddy paw prints, else there will be a lot of trouble for both of us. I can't hide you here, I wish I could but if anyone finds you they will kick you straight out again. Meet me here at the same time tomorrow by the picture of Saint Barbara. Careful that no one sees you. This time, I'll bring some table scraps for you to eat.'

Thomas was very sad to be leaving the church and Maude. He'd had the most wonderful time playing with her; she was his only friend in all the world and the idea of going back out on to the street after all that was devastating. But Thomas took courage at the thought of seeing her again. It was enough courage to see him through a horrible night on the cold and blustery street.

The next day at the same time he returned to their meeting place and sure enough, Maude was waiting for him by the picture of Saint Barbara. They had lots of fun playing together; Maude invented a new game where Thomas had to outrun her broom and, later, he ate the table scraps she brought for him. How lovely to have food inside his belly. Then it was time for him to go back out on the streets but they promised to meet in the same spot the following day. And sure enough, the next day there she was. And the day after that. And the day after that. And the day after that. Every day they waited for each other by the picture of Saint Barbara and every day they played together and shared table scraps when no one else was around.

Until, one day, little Maude wasn't there. She wasn't there the day after. Or the day after. Thomas continued to wait for her faithfully by the picture of Saint Barbara but after the third day of waiting he began to consider with a very heavy heart that she wasn't going to come for him any more.

Just then, all of a sudden, he heard footsteps running down the church nave. It was Maude! Thomas ran towards her and sprang delightedly into her arms. Maude nuzzled his fur up to her face and Thomas noticed that her cheeks were all wet. Maude had been crying. But why?

'Oh I'm so glad you are still here,' she sniffed with tears rolling from her eyes. 'It's time for me to say goodbye now. I may be gone for a very long time because I have to leave Norwich and go to the countryside. The priest has secured me a job as a serving maid at a big manor house. I suppose I should be grateful but, oh I will miss you. You've been my best friend when I had no one to talk to. I wish I could take you with me but, oh dear, they already have all the cats they need to catch rats at the big manor. Or they might think you're a witch's friend and cast you out. I don't want that.'

She put Thomas gently down on the floor. 'I will come back for you though,' she said determinedly. 'I promise. Wait for me here by the picture of Saint Barbara. I will come and fetch you one day.'

Thomas looked up at her sadly. 'Goodbye Maude,' he sobbed. 'I will miss you!' though of course all she heard was 'meow'.

Then an adult came to take Maude away and Thomas hid behind the screen again so he wouldn't be seen. He heard footsteps fading down the nave towards the end of the church and by the time he came out, she was gone.

But she had promised to come back. He would wait for her here, every day, just as he had always done until she came to fetch him. Every day, Thomas waited by the picture of Saint Barbara. The days turned into weeks. The weeks turned into months. The months turned into years. Thomas didn't know how much time had passed, only that seasons came and went and that he was growing much bigger. One day he caught sight of himself in a puddle of water on the ground and realised that he was a fully grown cat. He thought it must have been a very long time since last he saw Maude and she had probably forgotten all about him by now. It seemed silly to carry on waiting. She had a new life now. There would surely be lots of people at the big manor house in the countryside. She didn't need friends like him any more. Still, there was always that glimmer of hope. And so, Thomas continued to go every day at the same time to the picture of Saint Barbara and wait for Maude. Day after day, he waited and waited.

One particularly cold, dreary and windy day Thomas was curled up in a ball next to the picture of Saint Barbara sleeping gently on and off. He was very tired that day. He had found of late that his legs, which once could run and run and run, weren't quite as nimble as they used to be. His eyes, which once could spot people coming a mile off, weren't quite as sharp as they used to be. His nose, which could smell food from down the street, wasn't quite as keen as it used to be. And he needed to sleep much more frequently than he used to.

Thomas was worried he might fall asleep and overstay his welcome to the time when the church became busy again, so he decided to hide behind the rood screen in the chancel. He had just curled up in a ball on the other side of the panel when he heard a voice from the other side of the church. His ears pricked up, though again, not quite as sharply as they used to.

'What's this?' said the voice. 'Little paw prints across the floor.'

Alarmed, Thomas looked down at his feet and realised that they were covered in mud. He must have left a trail and now whoever that voice belonged to, they were going to find him!

'One, two, three …' the person was counting his paw prints.

'Four, five, six, seven …' the voice didn't sound angry or cross. It sounded quite warm and friendly. But his heart sank with the realisation that it couldn't possibly be Maude coming back for him after all these years, the voice was much too different.

'Eight, nine, ten!' The next thing Thomas knew, he was face to face with … no, it couldn't be! Maude? But she wasn't little any more. She was quite tall. Her face looked different, it was bigger and redder and her hair was scraped back over her head in a piece of white cloth. Her dress was still plain but she wasn't covered in dirt the way she used to be.

But of course, just as Thomas had grown, so had Maude. She was much older now, which was why she looked and sounded different.

Maude beamed an enormous smile. 'It's you!' She picked Thomas up and swung him around in her arms.

Thomas was so happy that she had come back for him, just like she promised. He purred and purred and purred. Then, from over her shoulder, Maude called out, 'It's him! He's still here!' and from behind her there appeared another figure. Thomas shrank back a little because he was scared of getting caught.

'It's alright,' Maude assured him. 'You've nothing to be scared of here. This is my husband Peter, he's a pastry cook from the big manor. And this is my little Alfred.'

Thomas saw that the figure was a man. He was smiling an enormous smile, and in his arms he held a baby. So Maude had got married and had a baby! And now she had come back for him as well.

'Peter and I have enough money to make our own home now,' said Maude. 'But we couldn't go anywhere without coming back for you.' She squeezed Thomas tightly. 'And now we are all a family.'

Thomas had never felt so happy as Maude carried him in her arms down the church alongside Peter and Alfred the baby. Before they left and headed to their new home there was just one last thing he had do.

From over Maude's shoulder Thomas could still see the picture of Saint Barbara on Saint Gregory's rood screen. She had been his home for so long. She had brought him and Maude together and now, after all this time, she had reunited them.

Thomas waved a paw at the picture. 'Thank you! Goodbye!'

ERIC AND THE EXTRAORDINARY STATUE

The Statue of Samson From the Samson and Hercules Duo

Last Tuesday afternoon in the Museum of Norwich at the Bridewell, something extraordinary happened to a boy called Eric.

Eric wasn't the sort of boy who was used to extraordinary things happening to him, quite simply because it wasn't in his nature to go round looking for them to happen. You see, Eric 'liked to keep himself to himself', at least that's what other people said about him. He was often described as a 'quiet' sort of a boy, one who didn't easily come out of his shell.

It wasn't that Eric especially liked being on his own. On the contrary, he enjoyed the company of other people and, if he did talk, would tell you there were lots of people he found very interesting, friendly, warm, smart and funny. It's just that words didn't come all that naturally to Eric and he tended to shy away from conversation. Instead, he preferred to draw pictures.

Eric was a fantastic artist. He always kept a notebook and pencil on him and liked to draw anything that caught his eye. He could draw really fast without even blinking. When he drew, it was almost as if the hand holding his pencil was a separate part of his body that moved with unbelievable speed, as though under a magical spell. Eric would happily draw any picture you asked him to. *Draw a bike, Eric, or a really fast car. Draw my breakfast or a beautiful dress. Draw a talking elephant or a dancing hippopotamus.* No request was too silly for Eric. You name it, he would draw it.

So you see, in this way Eric was a very chatty person but the way he chatted was different.

Last Tuesday afternoon, around the time the extraordinary thing happened to Eric, he was on a school trip with his Class 3B and their teacher, Miss Roberts. They were looking at all the wonderful and curious objects in the Museum of Norwich at the Bridewell. Eric never talked to anyone in his class and so had spent most of the day shuffling around on his own at the back of the group, drawing pictures in his notebook.

In an upstairs room of the museum, Miss Roberts gathered the class in a small crowd in front of a very tall and unusual-looking statue.

The statue was of an enormous man. The man was very bulky, very big and looked extremely strong. His face was large and serious with a heavy set nose from which protruded a bushy moustache. At the top of his nose rested two thick slits for eyes and above these, a stern-looking forehead. His head was covered with long hair which flowed down to his shoulders. He was wearing some very funny clothes. They were robes which draped from his shoulders and hung above his knees. The rest of his legs were bare and his feet were two large boulder-like blocks, standing solidly on the ground. You wouldn't want him to step on your foot, thought Eric, he'd be bound to break a bone or two!

In his left hand the statue held a small animal which looked like a little fox. It was an oddly tender sight; this tiny creature curled up in the statue's muscular sturdy hand and Eric felt as though the statue may be looking after or protecting it. In his right hand, which was held up to his shoulder, was an enormous club. Crikey, thought Eric, he could give you a mighty wallop with that!

'This statue is called Samson,' Miss Roberts explained. 'He is made of wood. The creature in his arm, as you might have guessed, is a fox and you see that huge club he is holding? Well, it isn't actually a club; it may look a bit like one but it's really the jawbone of an ass or, as we call them, a donkey. Samson didn't always stand alone. He had a friend called Hercules and the two statues stood outside Samson and Hercules House which is on a street called Tombland. The two figures are very famous to Norwich.'

'Please Miss,' asked a girl from Eric's class. 'What exactly *is* he? I mean, is he a man?'

Miss Roberts smiled. 'You're quite right to question what he is exactly as I'm sure you've never seen anything like him before. Samson is indeed a man. He is based on an old ancient story about two very strong and fearsome men who were expert hunters and fighters. It may seem strange that they are such famous figures in a friendly place like Norwich. But today, they represent a sense of protection, of guarding the city and those within it. I think that makes them very magical indeed.'

Eric agreed that there was something most magical about the statue and he wanted to draw Samson right away. He gripped his pencil and notebook which were at his side.

'Now class,' said Miss Roberts. 'Follow me downstairs. There are a few more things on the ground floor that I want us to see.'

She led the way to a set of stairs opposite to where Samson stood and the class followed. But Eric stayed behind. He just needed a few minutes to draw the statue alone. Once everyone was gone, faster than a flash, Eric drew Samson in his notebook. He was a terrific challenge to draw because he was so enormous and peculiar. At last Eric thought he had captured him spot on. Satisfied, he was about to close his notebook when he heard sniggering from behind him.

Eric turned around slowly and saw that a group of boys from his class were standing at the top of the stairs and that they were all laughing at him. They must have been standing there the whole time, thought Eric, and he felt a horrible lump in his stomach as he realised they had been laughing all that while behind his back when he thought he was alone.

It was the same group that were always making fun of him whenever he drew anything. Eric never really understood why; it wasn't as if he was doing anything particularly funny. All he was doing was drawing in a book. What was their problem? Still, he couldn't help but wish he was tough enough to stand up to them. It was all he could do to hold his head in his hands with embarrassment as the boys clumped back down the stairs and he heard their footsteps and laughter fade away. This time, Eric really was alone. He felt dejected and humiliated. Why did he have to be different? Why did he insist on drawing everything instead of talking like the other boys? Eric resolved that as soon as he got back home, he would throw his notebook away and never draw anything ever again.

'Don't be downhearted, dear boy!'

Eric started at the sound of a man's booming voice. He looked up from his hands and jumped back in shock as he saw that Samson, yes the statue Samson, was standing right next to him, looking over his shoulder at the notebook. But this couldn't be happening. Eric took a few alarmed steps back but Samson only moved further forward. His movements were as clumpy and stumpy as you might expect for an enormous statue and his feet made a resounding 'thud' each time they hit the ground. Eric only realised now that he was right up close how much taller Samson was than himself. It was very unnerving to see Samson's head looming so far above his own.

'What a wonderful picture you've drawn of me!' Samson said. His mouth opened very wide indeed when he spoke and his voice was loud and bellowing. 'I must congratulate you on your artistic talent. You really have captured my likeness most exquisitely. Why, I look positively handsome, dare I say, dashing?'

Although Eric was frankly terrified by the sight of a talking, walking statue, he couldn't help but laugh at how jolly and friendly Samson seemed to be. He really did seem genuinely delighted with the picture Eric had drawn. It was quite odd, considering he had a somewhat ferocious appearance.

'Sorry for making you jump, dear boy,' Samson said. 'I understand that you may be a little thrown by the sight of my coming to life.

I don't usually do it you know, unless I see a terrible injustice.'

'Oh,' said Eric in a whisper. 'What sort of injustice?'

For a boy who didn't talk much to anyone, Eric certainly wasn't used to talking to strangers let alone statues that had come to life. But the circumstances were so bizarre that he felt he absolutely had to say something, almost as though the words were coming out of his mouth and he was helpless to stop them.

'What sort of injustice?' Samson repeated startled. 'Why the sight of those awful boys making fun of you, of course, when all you were doing was simply drawing that dazzling picture of me!' He beamed a huge smile down at Eric. 'Do you know why I think they make fun of you?'

Eric shook his head because he really didn't know.

'They're jealous,' said Samson. 'You mark my words on it lad. They wish that they could draw as marvellously as you can.'

Eric looked down at his feet. 'It doesn't feel that way,' he said sadly. 'I wish I could stick up to them, only sometimes I think they must be right to make fun of me because I don't really have any friends.'

'Oh, but you will, dear boy,' assured Samson. 'You just haven't come out of your shell yet. But when you do, you'll make friends sure enough. I'm certain that lots of people will like you and will be mightily impressed by your gift for drawing. After all, there's nothing wrong with being a little different.'

'Oh, I'm sure that's the case,' mumbled Eric. 'It's just that, I can't help but feel rather lonely sometimes.'

'Well,' said Samson 'I'll let you in on a secret. Sometimes I get lonely too. I used to have a best friend and we stood beside each other always and forever.'

'You mean Hercules?' asked Eric.

'Yes! Hercules, you've heard of him!' cried Samson with evident delight. 'My most excellent best friend! We stood together outside Samson and Hercules House for hundreds of years!'

'I would love to see you standing together outside the house,' said Eric.

'Oh, would you?' Samson looked at Eric with a glint in his eyes. 'Well, why don't I show you?'

The next thing Eric knew, *whoosh!* He was standing somewhere completely different. Eric had no idea how that happened. One second he was inside the museum, the next second he wasn't.

'How did you do that?' he asked Samson.

'Well I'm no wizard or what have you,' Samson smiled. 'But I do have a few tricks up my sleeve. Now, have a look around and see where you are.

Eric looked around him. He and Samson were standing outside a building on a street. It was Samson and Hercules House and the street must have been in Tombland! Eric could tell this straight away because the building had a front porch with four steps leading up to it and on either side of the porch stood two enormous statues which supported the roof of the porch, like pillars. Samson and Hercules standing together as they would have been! Eric saw that the one on the left was Samson. That meant the one on the right must have been Hercules.

'He looks quite similar to me, doesn't he?' Samson remarked fondly. 'Though can you spot how he is different?'

Eric saw that Hercules had the same large, round, bulging shape. He too had long, flowing hair, robes that hung from his shoulders to his knees and large clumpy feet. However, unlike Samson he wasn't holding an animal in his hands. Instead, his left arm crossed over to his right shoulder in which he held an enormous club. Across his right shoulder he appeared to be wearing a lion skin.

'We're both dressed very fiercely, aren't we?' remarked Samson. 'That's because it's our job to guard the building so we need to look a bit rough and tough so as to scare off anyone who might mean harm. We stood here for hundreds of years! Now, standing in the same spot for so long may sound a bit boring to you but on the contrary it was wildly entertaining. We've seen plenty of wondrous things that happened in Norwich. If you turn around you'll see that Norwich Cathedral is directly in front of us.'

Eric turned away from the statues and saw a huge, magnificent building with lots of pointy turrets in front of him. The entrance to the building was a very grand doorway in an arch shape. He and Samson went and stood at the top of the four steps so that they could get a good view.

'Lots of exciting things have happened outside the cathedral over the years and we were in a prime spot to view them!'

'What sort of things?' asked Eric.

All of a sudden, *whoosh!* There appeared from nowhere a large procession of people. They all looked very happy and joyful and were dancing in a huge group in front of the cathedral. Eric saw lots of colour, laughter, music and noise – it was a very jolly sight.

'Where did all these people come from?' asked Eric. 'Can they see us?'

'No,' said Samson, 'these people are from a memory of mine which happened a very, very long time ago. They can't see us but isn't it wonderful that we can see them! Let's stay here at the top of these steps and watch what happens.'

Eric saw that leading the procession was a very spectacular sight: a dragon. He jumped back in disbelief. A real dragon? No, it must have been a person wearing a dragon costume because the dragon only had two legs. Still, it was very lifelike. The dragon was red, green and gold with a rather fierce-looking face and a pointy jaw, wide open revealing many sharp silver teeth.

Lots of children were dancing around the dragon though Eric couldn't help but feel it looked a bit scary and he wouldn't want to get too close. Every now and then the dragon would slap his jaws together which would make a snapping sound. Rather than frighten the children, they seemed to find this very funny and would run right up to him as though daring themselves to get close, then run away laughing when he snapped his jaws together.

'That's the famous Norwich Snap Dragon,' said Samson. 'He's called Snap because of the snapping sound his jaw makes. All these people dancing and prancing about are here for the Guild Day procession which was a celebration held on the streets here for hundreds of years. It was a very fun and happy day for all involved.'

Eric was absolutely fascinated by the dragon and quickly began to draw him in his notebook. No sooner had he completed his drawing then all of a sudden *whoosh!* The Norwich Snap Dragon and Guild Day procession disappeared and in their place was a different sight in front of Norwich Cathedral.

Again the street was busy. Lots of people were gathered together and there was a feeling of great anticipation in the air, as though something very important was about to happen.

'Why are all these people here?' asked Eric.

'They are here to witness the unveiling of the statue of a woman called Edith Cavell,' said Samson. 'Edith Cavell is very famous to the people of Norwich because she was born here and went on to do many brave and heroic things during the time of a terrible war. Edith was a nurse who helped soldiers to get better. Not only that but she helped them to escape the enemy. Very courageous woman. This statue is to commemorate her memory.'

Suddenly there was a gasp from the crowd. Eric looked to see what they were gasping at and saw that a man had drawn a veil from over the top of the statue. The statue was the head of Edith Cavell which stood on a large stone. Carved on to the stone was a solider holding up a wreath. She must have been a very important woman, thought Eric, to have her own memorial statue outside Norwich Cathedral. If she had saved people's lives then it seemed right that she should be remembered.

Eric drew the statue in his notebook. No sooner had he drawn it then *whoosh!* Everything changed again.

This time it was dark. Eric looked up and saw that the night sky glittered with thousands of stars. There was a real buzz in the air and Eric got the feeling that something very inspiring was about to happen. Then all of a sudden a man walked up the steps of Samson and Hercules House and brushed right past Eric! The man was dressed very smartly in a suit and a huge crowd of people surrounded him as he made his way towards the front door.

'Who is he?' asked Eric. 'Why is he going inside Samson and Hercules House? And why are all those people following him?'

'There was once a time when Samson and Hercules House was a dance hall,' explained Samson, 'full of dancing and fun. Hercules and I witnessed a very famous musician walk up the steps of this porch to go and perform inside the house. His name was Glenn Miller – you may not have heard that name but at the time he was a huge star.'

Quickly, Eric drew the man in his notebook. Samson leaned over Eric's shoulder to look at his drawing. 'It's good to see that you are enthusiastically scribbling away my boy,' he said, 'considering how those boys treated you earlier and how downhearted you were. It's nice to see this hasn't discouraged you from drawing.'

Eric shrugged. 'It nearly did,' he said. 'But I don't think anything could ever stop me from drawing. There are just too many wonderful things in the world that need to be drawn. They can't put me off any more, they're just bullies. It's like you said Samson, there's nothing wrong with being a little different.'

No sooner had Eric said this then *whoosh!* They were back where they started in the upstairs room of the Museum of Norwich at the Bridewell.

'Wow,' said Eric. 'That was amazing. Thanks Samson ... Samson?'

But Samson said nothing. Because Samson was a statue. Just a statue standing still. Eric gaped at him in disbelief. Perhaps he had imagined the whole thing. After all, people were often telling him that he slipped into his own little dream world. Maybe that was the case in this instance. But then Eric remembered to look down at the notebook in his hands. They were still there! The pictures he had drawn of the Snap Dragon, the statue of Edith Cavell, and of Glenn Miller walking into the dance hall were all there. He couldn't possibly have imagined all those things, else why would he still have the pictures? Eric felt elated that Samson coming to life must have been real but, at the same time, very disappointed that his new friend was now just a statue again. He recalled that Samson said he only came to life when he saw a terrible injustice. Perhaps, thought Eric, there wasn't an injustice any more though he wasn't quite sure how it had been resolved.

Sadly, Eric trundled down the stairs to Miss Roberts and Class 3B on the ground floor.

Unfortunately for Eric, one of the boys who had been laughing at him earlier was waiting for him on the bottom step. He snatched the notebook from Eric's hands and opened it on the page of the Samson drawing. He held it out for the whole class to see.

'Hey guys, look at this! Look what Eric's been doing!' He flicked through the pages of the notebook and showed everyone the pictures of the Snap Dragon, the Edith Cavell statue and Glenn Miller. Eric took a deep breath and winced, fully expecting everyone to make fun too. What happened next came as a great and wonderful surprise. To his astonishment, Eric's class gathered round his notebook and all at once started to shout out, 'Wow! Did you draw those, Eric? Amazing! So lifelike! Incredible! Well done! Epic drawings, Eric.'

The boys who had bullied him all looked very embarrassed that the rest of the class weren't reacting in the way they wanted them to.

'What wonderful imagination you have, Eric,' Miss Roberts admired his drawing from the back of the group. 'Is that the Norwich

Snap Dragon I see? And the statue of Edith Cavell? And that one looks like Samson and Hercules House from back in its swinging dance hall days. If I didn't know any better I'd say you've drawn all the things that Samson and Hercules would have seen in their years of standing opposite Norwich Cathedral. What a clever idea. Well done you.'

Eric had never had so much praise in all his life. He felt immensely proud and found himself beaming from ear to ear. For the first time since he had started school, he spoke to his classmates.

'Thanks guys,' he said. 'You're the best.'

Needless to say, Eric had no problems making friends that day. You might even say that the bullies had helped with this matter, although Eric would tell you the person who really helped was Samson. He had found his own way of putting the terrible injustice to rights by encouraging Eric to draw all the things he had seen outside Samson and

Hercules House. He wanted Eric to feel proud of his drawings, not ashamed.

Of course, this only happened last Tuesday and Eric is still taking a while to come out of his shell. He is still often described as a 'quiet' boy who 'likes to keep himself to himself', but now Eric knows that no one minds at all. As Samson would say, 'There's nothing wrong with being a little different.'

The statue of Edith Cavell stands outside Norwich Cathedral to this day.

You can see Samson and Hercules stand outside Samson and Hercules House in Tombland. They are a delightful bright red!

You can visit the Samson statue in this story at the Museum of Norwich at the Bridewell.

THE
TOFFEE TWINS
Toffee Guillotine

This story is set rather a long time ago, when your great-grandparents or great, great-grandparents would have been around. Dorothy and Florence Millard lived with their mother and father in a house in the city of Norwich. No one ever actually called the girls Dorothy and Florence; instead they were known as Dorrie and Florrie. Indeed, if anyone ever did call the girls Dorothy and Florence both would burst out laughing because they weren't used to it at all and would usually end up mimicking the unfamiliar manner in which they were addressed.

'Oh I say, how do you do, Lady Dorothy?'

'Well, I say, I'm quite well thank you, Lady Florence.'

Dorrie and Florrie were identical twins; they looked exactly the same. It was impossible to tell them apart. Two heart-shaped faces. Two pairs of big brown eyes. Two sets of short black hair. Two cheeky smiles.

As they looked so similar, people would often get them muddled up. They would call

Dorrie, Florrie and Florrie, Dorrie. This was tremendous fun for the twins and they would often go along with it, sometimes for a whole day until the poor person in question realised that they were mistaken.

The trouble was that it was extremely difficult to tell one from the other because as well as being identical in looks, they were equally identical in personality.

Dorrie and Florrie liked exactly the same things. Both liked singing, skipping and playing the piano (badly). Both liked to be in the company of the other. Indeed, they were never apart, not only twins but the best of friends – the girls stuck together like glue.

Now, there's one important thing that Dorrie and Florrie had in common which you need to know about for this story and that thing was a sweet tooth. Luckily for the girls they lived in Norwich, as back then the city was very famous for making chocolate. Anyone visiting Norwich would have quickly noticed that the air was filled with a rich, enticing and distinctly chocolaty smell. Should they have traced where the smell was coming from they would have found themselves at a great big chocolate factory in the heart of Norwich, owned by a company called Mackintosh. Lots of people worked in this factory to make chocolate which tasted delicious, looked tempting and smelled lovely, ready to sell in shops. The twins loved to visit some of these shops so they could stare at the wonderful chocolate.

Now, as much as the twins enjoyed eating chocolate, their parents wouldn't let them eat it very often because they said that too much chocolate was bad for you. They were only allowed to have chocolate as a treat on very special occasions such as Christmas, Easter and their birthday, which of course, being twins, they shared.

Their birthday was particularly special because that was the day when Grandad visited. Grandad worked in the Mackintosh Factory and every year he would bring the twins chocolate from the factory as a birthday present. He always brought them the same chocolate in exactly the same amount and didn't dream of doing otherwise because he knew that one didn't want anything different from the other.

The chocolate birthdays happened every year up until the twins turned eight. That year, Grandad's birthday present changed because his job had changed. He still worked in the Norwich Mackintosh Factory but as well as chocolate, he helped to make a new sweet: toffee!

Grandad worked as an operator on a very special piece of equipment in the factory called a toffee guillotine. The job of the toffee guillotine was to cut up the slabs of toffee. For a machine which helped to make something so sweet, it looked a little bit scary. The toffee guillotine was a great big brown machine which came with instructions to be very careful because you could really hurt your fingers when using it if you weren't. In this way, you could say that Grandad's job of using the toffee guillotine wasn't without a dangerous streak. He had to practise and practise handling the machine before he finally got to grips with it. All that practise paid off because Grandad soon became an expert at running the machine.

Grandad had gone to so much effort learning how to use the toffee guillotine, he decided it would be a wonderful idea to bring the twins toffee instead of chocolate for their birthday, because he was proud of his work and wanted people to enjoy the results.

On the twins' eighth birthday, Grandad walked up to the house where they lived with two paper bags. Each contained three toffee slabs of exactly the same size for his granddaughters who liked everything the same.

It was a warm winter's afternoon and the air was beautifully crisp. It had been raining a little that morning but he managed to avoid the many puddles on his stroll up to the house. When he arrived, Grandad rang the doorbell and waited. He expected the door to fling open and to be bombarded as he usually was with two girls rushing gleefully towards him. This time, however, no one answered the door. Grandad rang the bell again. No answer. He rang again. Still no answer. He rang the bell again and finally it opened. But it wasn't the twins who greeted him – it was Mum.

'Hello!' Grandad greeted her with a big smile. Mum didn't smile back which was unusual because she was normally a very cheery, smiley sort of a person.

'You don't seem quite yourself,' said Grandad. 'Is everything alright?'

'Oh dear,' said Mum. 'I'm afraid it isn't.'

'What's wrong?' asked Grandad.

'It's the twins,' said Mum. 'They're, well, you'll see …' She opened the door for Grandad to come into the house. No sooner had he stepped inside than he heard shouting.

Opposite the doorway was a staircase and much to his surprise, Grandad saw Dorrie running down it looking very tearful and upset. Stamping along behind her was Florrie who looked very angry.

'That's *my* dress, it's *my* dress and you can't wear it!' shouted Florrie, her face all red and unsettled.

'No,' shouted back Dorrie, 'it's *my* dress, I put it on first.'

Grandad saw that the girls were both wearing exactly the same dress, a red one with a ribbon around the waist tied in a bow at the back.

But they always wore the same clothes so what on earth were they arguing about?

'Girls, girls!' exclaimed Mum. 'They're both your dresses, besides you love to have clothes that are the same. At least, you used to.'

'I don't want to wear clothes that are the same as Dorrie any more,' said Florrie. 'I want to wear my own dresses without having her copy me all the time.'

'I'm not copying you,' protested Dorrie. 'I put it on first!'

'Well I think you're both being very silly,' said Mum, 'and if there's any more arguing about the dresses then I'll take them right back to the shop.'

'She started it!' Florrie pointed at Dorrie.

'No I didn't, it was you!' Dorrie yelled at Florrie and stormed down the rest of the stairs into the living room.

'Dear me!' said Grandad. 'It seems I've come at a bad time. Still, I think I'll stay because I wanted to give the girls their birthday presents.'

He followed Florrie and Dorrie into the living room where they were both sitting on chairs facing each other, shoulders hunched in a huff.

'Now, whatever is going on here?' Grandad asked as he entered the room. 'You two stick together like glue, remember? Why are you getting all cross at each other?'

'I want to wear something different to Dorrie,' said Florrie. 'But she keeps copying me.'

'No I don't,' snapped Dorrie. 'I want to wear something different to you too. I put the dress on first, you're copying me!'

'No I'm not!'

'Yes you are!'

Florrie stuck her tongue out at Dorrie.

Dorrie stuck her tongue out at Florrie.

'See!' cried Florrie, 'copying everything I do!'

'Well, really,' said Grandad, 'this is a very odd turn of events. There was me thinking you loved the same things and here you are arguing because you want to be different! But don't let a dress come between you, there's nothing wrong with wanting to be different from each other but you can still both wear the same dress if you want to. Now, I've had quite enough of all this squabbling. I came here to give you your birthday presents but you can only have them if you promise to stop quarrelling about silly things.'

The girls quickly stopped pulling faces at each other and looked serious.

'We promise,' they nodded their heads sincerely.

Grandad handed the girls one paper bag each. The girls looked inside.

'Oh Grandad,' Florrie sounded curious. 'I thought you were going to bring us chocolate from the factory. What's this?'

'It's toffee,' said Grandad. 'We make toffee at the factory too and I thought you might like some. Have you ever tried it?'

The girls shook their heads.

'Well, why don't you try it now? But I'll let you in on a secret before you do. It's very, very chewy.'

The girls dipped their hands into the paper bags and pulled out one piece of toffee each. Both pieces were a shiny golden brown. Simultaneously, the twins put the toffee pieces into their mouths. Following this there was a good deal of silence. Chomp, chomp, chomp! Their mouths moved up and down, around and around in big circles as they ate the toffee. Whilst they were eating they looked at each other and smiled.

'What's it like, girls?' asked Grandad.

'Delicious,' said Florrie in-between mouthfuls, so it sounded like 'dishush'.

'Sweet,' said Dorrie, though it sounded like 'shwwwsht'.

After a while they swallowed the toffee, grinned at each other and at exactly the same time said, 'Sticky!'

Grandad laughed. 'You see, there you are enjoying the same thing and you're not arguing about it this time. Just because you want to be different sometimes it doesn't mean you can't still like the same things. And it turns out you both like toffee so that present was a great success. How marvellous.'

'Dorrie, your face looked funny when you were eating the toffee,' giggled Florrie.

'So did yours,' Dorrie grinned. 'Why don't you try some Grandad?'

'Oh, I've tried plenty,' Grandad said. 'But when I do eat it, my toffee face usually looks like this.' He moved his mouth round and round in large circular motions and he widened his eyes as big as they could go.

'Toffee face!' the girls could hardly contain themselves and collapsed into fits of laughter.

'What's all this laughing about?' Mum was standing at the door.

Grandad showed Mum his toffee face and she started laughing too.

'Right,' he said when they had all quite finished, 'I've got a wonderful idea. Let's go to the park.' He took the paper bags back from the girls and placed them in his jacket pocket. 'We'll save some for later.'

Grandad waited by the door downstairs whilst the girls put on their hats and coats which were, of course, matching, but the twins were so excited about going to the park he was relieved to find they no longer seemed to mind that their clothes were the same.

That was, until they were just about to leave through the front door and Florrie said, 'That's my hat Dorrie! You're wearing my hat!'

'Of course I am,' said Dorrie. 'Both our hats are the same.'

'Yes,' said Florrie, 'but my hat has a flower sewn at the side, I did it myself'

She pointed at a little red flower made from wool sewn into the side of the hat.

'They both have flowers!' said Dorrie. She pointed to a blue flower on Florrie's hat.

'Yes,' said Florrie, 'but this one is blue and mine is the red one because my favourite colour is red.'

'No, my favourite colour is red. This hat is mine!'

'It's mine!'

'It's mine!'

'Oh, for goodness' sake,' Grandad interrupted the girls, rather annoyed. 'Is it worth arguing about?' He swiped the hat from Dorrie's head and put it on his own head. 'How about I wear the hat with the red flower? How about that? Would that put an end to all your silliness?'

The girls stared at Grandad. He was wearing a hat that was much too small for his head with a flower sticking out of the side. For a moment they were silent and only blinked at him. Then, all of a sudden, they both burst out laughing.

'You look so funny, Grandad!'

After that, the girls quite forgot their argument; Grandad returned the hat to Dorrie's head and off they went to the park.

Grandad had made sure that the girls were both wearing nice sturdy boots, which was useful as there were lots of puddles from the morning's rain which lined their way. Despite the downpour, however, it was far from a gloomy day. The sun had come out and you could see rainbow colours reflected in the many puddles in their path.

Splash! Dorrie jumped in one of the puddles.

Sploosh! Florrie jumped in a puddle too.

The water sprang lightly up the side of their boots. They were only little puddles.

'Stop jumping in puddles, Florrie, that's what I'm doing, you can't do it too!'

'I can jump in puddles if I want to, Dorrie.'

'Now girls,' said Grandad, 'let's not argue about jumping in puddles.'

But the twins weren't listening. Before Grandad had time to say 'stop it!' they were running in front of each other in a frantic race trying to get to the next nearest puddle first.

'This one's *my* puddle!'

'No, it's *my* puddle!'

'Right, that's it!' cried Grandad and he dashed as fast as he could in front of the girls and towards the next puddle. Grandad was a very fast runner and he soon overtook the twins. He saw a huge puddle lying in the middle of their pathway and charged towards it. 'I'm going to jump in the next one before you two even have a chance to argue about it!'

'No, Grandad!' cried the twins. 'Don't jump in that one, can't you see it's …'

But it was too late. *Splash!*

Oh dear, poor Grandad. He was so busy trying to stop the twins from arguing, running towards the puddle at a mad pace, that he hadn't noticed this was quite the biggest puddle of them all. A very big puddle indeed – it went all the way up to his knees.

The girls stared at Grandad standing in the middle of an enormous puddle, a befuddled

look on his face as he realised what had happened. Then they burst out laughing.

Grandad started laughing too. 'We'd better make this walk to the park a brisk one so my trousers can dry off in the sun.'

The twins quite forgot their argument and off they went.

The rest of the day followed in a similar pattern. When they got to the park, the girls were continuously finding things to squabble about. Whenever they got into an argument or competition about something, Grandad would put an end to it all by doing something silly to show them how silly they were being.

On the see-saw they argued about who was going highest so Grandad sat in the middle of it, meaning that they were both stuck in mid-air.

When they played on the slide they argued about who could slide the fastest, so Grandad went down the slide and got wedged in the middle – he was a bit too wide for it.

When they played on the swings they argued about who could swing the highest, so Grandad sat on a swing and twirled the chains round and round, then span so fast that he yelled, 'I'm dizzy!'

The girls were quite giddy with laughter so Grandad suggested they should all sit down on the park bench and have a breather.

'Can you smell chocolate?' asked Grandad.

The girls nodded.

'Lovely sweet-smelling Norwich!' smiled Grandad. 'The smell comes from the factory where I make toffee. Speaking of which, let's go home and have some more shall we?'

Back home, the three of them were all snuggled up warm and dry in the living room. Grandad took out the paper bags of toffee from his coat pocket. He handed the girls another piece each. He joined them in doing their toffee faces even though he wasn't eating any.

'I'm sorry we quarrelled so much today, Grandad,' said Florrie out of the blue and much to his surprise. 'Especially as it was about little things.'

'Yes,' said Dorrie. 'We seem to do that a lot lately,' she added thoughtfully, 'that is, argue about things that don't really matter.'

'Oh,' said Grandad. 'Little things do matter a great deal, but there's no need to get cross at each other about it. For years I've made chocolate and it's been my favourite treat in all the world but now I make toffee and I like that just as much. It's nice to like something new but you can still enjoy the same things as before. It's similar with you two. You want to be different from each other and that's wonderful, but it doesn't mean you can't still like the same things. And no matter what, you'll always stick together like glue.'

'No we won't,' said Florrie.

'Not like glue,' said Dorrie.

'Oh no,' sighed Grandad. 'What have I started? Another silly argument?'

'No!' they grinned. 'We stick together like toffee!'

Grandad beamed a huge smile of relief.

They all did their toffee faces.

'Toffee face!'

LET'S GET CRACKING!
Caley's Christmas Crackers

This story begins, as all good fairy tales begin, with 'Once upon a time'.

Now, in truth, this story is not a fairy tale at all. Fairy tales are set in a mysterious time and this story is set in a very real time when your great, great-grandparents, or perhaps even your great, great, great-grandparents would have been around. But well, since this was a very, very long time ago, that still sounds rather mysterious.

Fairy tales are set in magical places which don't really exist but this story is set in a city called Norwich, which definitely does exist. But well, Norwich is a rather magical city.

Fairy tales tend to have fairies in them and in this story, there are no fairies. But well, there is a plucky little girl, every bit as feisty and fun and mischievous as you might imagine a fairy would be. Her name was Winifred Jones but everyone called her Winnie.

So, all things taken into account, it seems right that the story should begin with 'Once upon a time'.

Once upon a time, this plucky little girl called Winnie lived in the magical city of Norwich in a mysterious long time ago. Winnie lived in a house with her Mum and Dad. Now, one crisp, cold winter evening, Winnie and her parents wrapped up all warm in their winter clothes and boots and went to watch some fireworks. There were only a few days to go till Christmas and so the fireworks were part of a Norwich Christmas celebration.

Winnie had never seen anything like the fireworks before. They were powerful little rockets which whizzed up to the sky and exploded in bright, flashing lights. Best of all, she loved the noise they made: *whoosh*, *whizz*, *fizz*, *pop*, *bang*, *crack!*

'Whoosh, whizz, fizz, pop, bang, crack,' Winnie sang loudly as the family walked home. Now, it rather needs to be said here that the street the family lived on was quite a sleepy sort of a street. It was a quiet street and the neighbours were quiet people. Winnie didn't mind at all that she was surrounded by quiet people, only she did rather wish that everyone would talk to each other every once in a while or at least say 'hello!' In all the time she had lived on the street with her family, she had never heard anyone so much as exchange words as they all left their houses for work or school in the morning.

You see, Winnie was a very talkative little girl. In the morning when Dad took her to school and she could see all their neighbours in their front gardens or standing at their windows, Winnie loved nothing better than to chat and chat and chat about the day she'd had and the things she liked and what she'd had for breakfast to any of the neighbours who would care to listen. The trouble was, none of the neighbours ever really did care to listen. Sometimes, if she waved at them, they would wave back, but that was all that ever happened. Mum and Dad had told her that the neighbours were very nice people but they just didn't like to chat.

Winnie liked to get to know people and it did seem rather odd that she should live amongst so many neighbours and see them every day and not even know so much as their names. She had made up names for them. There was Old Granny Green Hat who lived in the house opposite. Winnie called her Old Granny Green Hat because she always wore a green hat on her head even when she was indoors! There was Mrs Lavender Locks who lived two doors down. Winnie called her Mrs Lavender Locks because she had beautiful long flowing ebony hair. The way it flowed about reminded Winnie of the way the lavender in their front garden swayed in the breeze. There was Mr and Mrs Carpenter who lived three doors down. Winnie called them Mr and Mrs Carpenter because they were always making things out of wood. In the summer, they would sit in their front garden with great big blocks of wood and make chairs and tables and you could always hear the sound of hammering and chiselling coming from their house. Finally, there was Old Mr Rose Bush who lived in the house with the roses round the door. He was forever outside in his front garden planting and growing things. He especially took great care with his rose bush, which was so big it was almost as big as his house. The bush was covered with lovely sweet-smelling red roses and Winnie got the feeling that it was his pride and joy.

It was good fun to make up pretend names for people but still, she would much rather have known what their proper names were.

'Quiet down, Winnie,' Mum said. 'This is a quiet street with quiet people. The neighbours don't want to hear you making whooshes and bangs and other funny noises!'

'But I'm so excited about the fireworks!' Winnie danced around as she spoke, 'I wish we had fireworks to play with at home!'

'Oh no you don't,' said Dad. 'Fireworks are very dangerous indeed. You must never play with fireworks. They are only for grown-ups who know how to use them safely. But if you like the noises they made, I'm sure we can find one or two things around the house that aren't dangerous and could make a similar sound.'

'This calls for an adventure!' cried Winnie. 'A quest to find things that sound like fireworks!'

'Yes, yes,' Mum and Dad said together, 'but you don't need to tell the whole world about it! This is a quiet street with quiet neighbours!'

Winnie saw some of the neighbours poke their heads outside their windows or doors. They looked a little grumpy.

'Whoosh, whizz, fizz, pop, bang, crack,' Winnie whispered to herself very quietly the rest of the way home.

Now, there was another resident at the family household: a dog called Buttons. Buttons was a big, bouncy dog with soft golden fur, floppy ears and a great big wet nose. Buttons hadn't gone out with the family that evening because dogs don't really like fireworks. Instead he had stayed at home and kept the house safe and sound for the family to return to. When they opened the front door, Buttons bounded up towards everyone gleefully.

'Buttons!' Winnie ran towards him, delighted as ever to see her lovely dog. 'I can't wait to tell you all about the fireworks, Buttons, and the amazing noises they made ... whoosh, whizz ...'

'Yes, before you get carried away young lady, you need to get ready for bed,' Mum said.

Winnie got ready for bed. Before she got into bed she went to find Buttons who was settled down in the kitchen and curled her arms around him.

'The fireworks went whoosh, whizz, fizz, pop bang, crack,' Winnie told a very interested Buttons. 'It was so much fun! Tomorrow, we're going on an adventure – a quest to find things that sound like fireworks!'

Buttons gave a yelp of joy swiftly followed by a great big yawn because he was tired and it was time for them both to go to bed.

The next morning, Winnie woke up feeling very excited. Today was going to be a fun, adventurous day! Winnie sprang out of bed, got washed and dressed then went downstairs to the kitchen for breakfast. Now, most people like to walk down the stairs but Winnie preferred to slide down the banister. Wheeee!

Whilst she was eating breakfast she heard Mum and Dad talking in rather excited voices at the kitchen door. What was going on?

In his hands, Dad was holding a large box. 'Winnie,' he announced. 'Mum and I were saving these for Christmas Day and though it's a little early yet, we wanted to give these to you now because you liked the fireworks so much. Well, you can't play with fireworks but you can play with these.'

Dad opened the box. Winnie looked inside. She saw a collection of brightly coloured funny-looking little objects. Each was a small tube that looked as though it was made out of shiny foil. They were red, green, pink, blue, purple and orange.

It was such a jolly and colourful sight, it seemed to Winnie as though someone had wrapped up a rainbow in a box. She was filled with curiosity as to what the rainbow objects were.

'They are called Caley's Christmas Crackers,' Dad answered her thoughts.

Winnie giggled. She had never heard of something called a 'cracker' before – what a funny name!

'You know how I work for a company called Caley's up at the big factory in Chapelfield? Well, I help to make these. This Christmas, the company have let me take a few home for my family.'

Dad took out a cracker from the box. 'Now, if I pull at one end and you pull at the other end, the cracker will break in half and as it does it makes a bang sound, a bit like the fireworks. It might even make you jump a bit. Not only that but inside the cracker, you'll find a little toy. But you won't know what it is till you've opened the cracker – it's a surprise!'

'That sounds so much fun!' cried Winnie.

'Yes,' said Dad, 'it is. But listen, these crackers are a real treat for everyone to enjoy at Christmas time. There are quite a few crackers in this box and I was going to save them all but well, since you have such an inquisitive mind that seems to find wonder in everything and you were so fascinated by the fireworks last night, your Mum and I wanted you to be able to play with these today. You may take five from the box and that should keep you going!'

'Oh, thank you!' said Winnie. She was so thrilled that the crackers made noises like fireworks. She couldn't wait to play with them and after breakfast, took the five crackers straight to Buttons.

Buttons was sitting in the living room, looking out of the big front window. You could see the whole street from the big front window and all the houses belonging to the neighbours that they never talked to.

'Listen carefully, Buttons,' Winnie knelt beside her beloved dog. 'We're going to have a super fun day playing with crackers that go bang just like the fireworks.'

But Buttons didn't look as pleased about that as she hoped he would. Instead, his face was drooping and he looked a little bit down in the dumps.

'Whatever is wrong, Buttons?' Winnie asked. Buttons nudged his head towards the window and Winnie followed his gaze. Outside it had started to snow gently. Snow was a very magical thing so she didn't know why Buttons would be downhearted. But then, Winnie saw what Buttons was looking at. She could see directly into the front window of the opposite house where Old Granny Green Hat was sitting in her rocking chair, wearing her green hat as usual. She was all on her own and looked rather sad.

'It must get quite lonely to live on a street where no one ever talks to each other,' Winnie said sadly. 'I wonder if she has anyone to spend Christmas with?'

She looked down at her collection of crackers. 'It seems a shame for us to play with all these toys when other people might like them too.'

Suddenly, Winnie sprang to her feet, full of energy. 'I've got a much better idea for our adventure today, Buttons. We're going to say hello to the neighbours on the street, the ones we never talk to. We're going to bring them some whoosh, whizz, fizz, pop, bang, crack! Come on Buttons!'

Buttons stopped looking blue and barked with excitement. Winnie went to the front door and put on her big, sturdy boots, her warm winter coat and completed the outfit with her hat, scarf and gloves. She told Mum and Dad that she was taking Buttons for a walk, to wish Happy Christmas to the neighbours and wouldn't go any further than three doors down.

Winnie didn't have a bag to put the five crackers in so instead, she used a little wooden wheelbarrow that she'd been given as a birthday present. Winnie loved to help with the gardening, especially in the spring when everything started to blossom and come to life. She loved to plant seeds and watch them grow and she often helped to dig up earth, so a wheelbarrow had been the perfect present.

Winnie went to the garden shed in the family's little back garden, got out her wheelbarrow and wheeled it around the back door with the five crackers inside to the street at the front of the house where Buttons was waiting for her.

'Right Buttons,' she said. 'Let's get cracking!'

Off went Winnie through the snowy street pushing her wheelbarrow of five crackers, Buttons bounding at her side.

First, they went to Old Granny Green Hat's house.

Winnie knocked on the door. After a short while, Old Granny Green Hat answered it.

Winnie wasn't quite sure what she had been expecting but she had somewhat thought that Old Granny Green Hat would be happy to see them and was a little taken aback that the old woman seemed quite grumpy and irritable at seeing her and Buttons on her doorstep.

'What do you want?' Old Granny Green Hat snapped and she raised a rather cross eyebrow at Winnie and Buttons. Buttons looked down and shuffled his paws awkwardly.

'I'm erm ... sorry if I interrupted anything,' stumbled Winnie anxiously. 'Only I wanted to bring you a Christmas cracker.'

'Eh?' Old Granny Green Hat said. 'A Christmas what?'

'Cracker,' said Winnie and she took out a cracker from the wheelbarrow and held it out to Old Granny Green Hat. 'If you pull the other side it goes bang and inside there's a surprise toy. I want you to have it.'

'Now listen,' said Old Granny Green Hat somewhat strictly. 'I don't know if this is some sort of joke but I would like you to leave and kindly stop bothering me.'

Winnie's heart sank as she realised that Old Granny Green Hat thought that she and Buttons were being a nuisance. But it wasn't on purpose! Winnie thought she should try to explain herself.

'I really don't want to bother you at all,' Winnie said. 'It's only that my Dad makes Caley's Christmas Crackers for his job and he's given me some to play with. Well, I thought it would be nice to share them because people on this street don't normally talk to each other. But I love sharing things and talking too so I thought it would be nice to say hello and give you a cracker and talk to you and say hello and talk and give you a cracker and say hello …' Winnie trailed off nervously, realising that the more she went round and round in circles, the more Old Granny Green Hat's face looked disapproving.

'Oh, alright then,' Old Granny Green Hat sighed at last. 'If that's really why you're here, let's pull the cracker then.'

She took hold of the other end of the cracker. Winnie pulled. Old Granny Green Hat pulled. They pulled and pulled and pulled. Then all of a sudden …

Bang! The cracker snapped in half. Winnie took a jump back. Old Granny Green Hat took a jump back. Winnie couldn't help but smother a giggle when she realised that the cracker had made them both jump.

'Oh,' said Old Granny Green Hat. 'I wasn't expecting that.' She looked down at the cracker in her hand. Winnie was pleased to see that Old Granny Green Hat was holding the bigger half, which should contain the surprise toy inside.

'You should have a toy inside!' said Winnie. 'But like I said, I don't want to bother you any more. I just wanted to pull a cracker. Thank you! Goodbye.'

Winnie skipped off quickly with her wheelbarrow and Buttons hurried after her. She didn't want to bother Old Granny Green Hat any more. She was just happy that they had shared a cracker together and it had gone bang like a firework. It did seem rather a shame though that Old Granny Green Hat hadn't wanted to chat. Winnie would have loved to have found out her real name. Before she set off down the road, she took a peek back at the house to see if Old Granny Green Hat was still grumpy. Much to her delight, through the front window she saw that Old Granny Green Hat was looking at the cracker in her hand and smiling from ear to ear. She still looked a little confused and it was a surprised sort of a smile, but a smile nonetheless.

'I wonder what her surprise toy was?' Winnie said. 'She must like it though because she's smiling. That's nice! Right, come on Buttons, let's get cracking!'

And off went Winnie through the snowy street, pushing her wheelbarrow of four crackers, Buttons bounding at her side.

The next house Winnie stopped at was the house two doors down where Mrs Lavender Locks lived. The snow was falling softly on to the lawn at the front of the house. Winnie saw little footprints in the snow so it looked as though children had been playing in the garden not too long before she had arrived. This was odd because she hadn't known there were any other children living on the street. Winnie knocked on the blue door. After a while it opened and standing in the open doorway was Mrs Lavender Locks.

Mrs Lavender Locks was wearing a long apron that was covered in flour. She had flour on her hands and face too; there was even some flour in her lovely lavender locks! Winnie could tell that she was very tired; even though her eyes were shining and she seemed happy, there was a slightly exhausted expression on her face, almost as if she'd been running around all day and hadn't stopped to sit down once. Mrs Lavender Locks smiled a warm smile at Winnie.

'Hello little girl on my doorstep,' she said. Suddenly Buttons bounced up and Mrs Lavender Locks laughed, 'and hello to you too! What can I do for you both?'

Winnie felt a bit nervous after her encounter with Old Granny Green Hat. She didn't want to bother anyone. But Mrs Lavender Locks didn't seem to mind at all so Winnie cleared her throat and said, 'Hello! My name is Winnie, this is my dog Buttons and we live two doors down. I came to say hello and to give you this Christmas cracker because it's Christmas and I like to share things.' She took a Christmas cracker out of her wheelbarrow and held it out to Mrs Lavender Locks. 'The way it works, you see, if you pull on one end and I pull on the other end, it will snap in half and make a noise like fireworks and there's a surprise toy inside and it's for you to keep.'

'Goodness me,' said Mrs Lavender Locks, 'how wonderful, I've never heard of anything like that before. I'm sure my two children would enjoy this,' and she called out, 'Percy! Edith!'

All of a sudden, a little boy and a little girl appeared at Mrs Lavender Locks' side. The boy looked about Winnie's age and the girl, slightly younger. Just like Mrs Lavender Locks, they were both covered in flour too.

They must have been the children whose footprints were in the snow. How very odd that she should never have known there were other children living on the street!

'You must excuse us all for being covered in flour,' said Mrs Lavender Locks. 'We've been baking mince pies. They should be ready by tomorrow. It's shocking really that we've lived on this street two doors down from you for so long and never spoken but now I know that you are Winnie and Buttons and you know that these are my children, Percy and Edith. Oh, and my name is Mrs Newnham.'

Winnie gasped. She couldn't believe that she finally knew Mrs Lavender Locks' real name.

'I'm always so very busy being rushed off my feet what with having these two to look after,' said Mrs Newnham. 'But I'm so pleased you've popped round so we can have a chance to meet properly. Now, let's give this cracker a try.'

They pulled the cracker and everyone laughed when it went *bang!* Winnie gave Mrs Newnham another cracker from her collection for Percy and Edith to play with.

'I've got plenty more at home,' Winnie said, 'so you can keep the surprise toys.'

Winnie left feeling very encouraged that the Newnham family had liked the crackers. 'Right, come on Buttons, we've still got two houses to visit, let's get cracking!'

And off went Winnie through the snowy street, pushing her wheelbarrow of two crackers, Buttons bounding at her side.

The next stop was Mr and Mrs Carpenter's house. Winnie wasn't surprised to find that the two had been very busy making things from wood inside the house.

'We're making a toy train for our nephew to play with. He's not been very well recently so we're off to pay a visit to him later this afternoon.'

'I'm sorry he hasn't been very well,' said Winnie. 'If you give him one of these crackers, it's got a surprise toy inside,' and she gave them one of her crackers from the wheelbarrow, 'with love from Winnie and Buttons.'

Mr and Mrs Carpenter were delighted with the gift. 'Oh, and if you call again,' they said, 'we are Mr and Mrs Lewis. Thank you, Winnie and Buttons!'

The next stop was the house with the roses round the door.

Old Mr Rose Bush was very pleased with his Christmas cracker. 'I'm very flattered that you should give me the last cracker from your wheelbarrow,' he said. 'You must come round and see my garden in the summer when the rose bush is in full bloom. I can't do any gardening what with this snow but I've taken to growing pot plants instead.'

He showed Winnie a little red rose that he was growing in a pot. He was so friendly that Winnie thought it would be funny to tell him that she used to call him Old Mr Rose Bush. He chuckled and chuckled to hear that.

'Well,' he said, 'my real name is Mr Smith but I think Old Mr Rose Bush sounds much more grand. I'm very proud of my beautiful garden and all the plants that grow. Now, I do think it's time that you went home where it's warm because the snow is really starting to come down.'

He was right. The snow was beginning to fall very fast now in great big flakes from the sky.

And so, off went Winnie through the snowy street pushing her empty wheelbarrow, Buttons bounding at her side. There wasn't quite as much spring in his step now as he was feeling rather tired.

Back home, she and Buttons snuggled up all cosy in the living room and watched the snow fall from the front window.

'That was a very adventurous day, Buttons,' said Winnie. 'To think that after all this time, we've learned what everyone's names are!'

'Oh, everyone that is, except Old Granny Green Hat.' Across the road, she saw Old

Granny Green Hat in her rocking chair. 'I do hope we brightened up her day without being too much of a bother.'

The next day was Christmas Eve. It was mid-morning and Winnie was in the kitchen planning how she could make it to the moon with just a cardboard box and a wooden spoon. Mum and Dad were also in the kitchen making a cup of tea. Buttons was in the living room in his usual spot looking out of the front window. Then, all of a sudden, there came a knock at the door. Buttons instantly bounded up to the door enthusiastically and started to bark. Winnie followed Mum and Dad to the door to see who it was.

It was Mrs Newnham, Percy and Edith. They were holding a plate of mince pies. Winnie thought the pies looked scrummylicious. They were all golden brown and piled high on the plate.

'Hello,' said Mrs Newnham to Mum and Dad. 'And hello Winnie and Buttons too! I wanted to come round and introduce myself. My name is Mrs Newnham and these are my two children, Percy and Edith. Yesterday, Winnie was kind enough to come round our house and share her Christmas crackers with us. It was such a lovely surprise and made me think how I've always been so very busy I've not yet made the time to come and talk to the neighbours. So, here we are and I think it's our turn to share something with you.' She held out the plate of mince pies. 'It seems very odd that we've been neighbours on the street for all these years and never really talked so I do hope you can enjoy these mince pies baked by the Newnham family two doors down!'

'Oh thank you,' said Mum. 'We're the Jones family. These mince pies look just delicious and there's certainly a lot of them! We're just having a cup of tea at the moment – would you like to come in for one and we'll all try these together?'

'That would be lovely,' said Mrs Newham. They all went inside to the kitchen. Buttons was very happy to see Percy and Edith again. New friends for him to play with!

No sooner had they all sat down for a cup of tea than there came a knock at the door again. Buttons sprang straight to the door and Mum, Dad, Winnie, Mrs Newnham, Percy and Edith followed.

It was Mr and Mrs Lewis. Mr Lewis was holding a wooden toy train in his hands.

'Hello,' said Mr Lewis cheerfully. 'We're Mr and Mrs Lewis. We wanted to pop round to say hello! Your little girl came round our house yesterday to share one of her Christmas crackers with us. Our little nephew was unwell and she said that he could keep the cracker. It was very kind! It seems only right that we should bring her a present in return.'

He bent down towards Winnie and handed her the wooden toy train.

'We made this for you along with the train for our nephew yesterday. Do you like trains?'

'I love trains!' cried Winnie, overjoyed with her new gift. 'I went on a train once with Mum and Dad. It was really fast and so much fun and it makes a noise like choo choo!' Everyone laughed.

'Winnie has a fondness for things that make very loud noises,' smiled Dad.

They invited Mr and Mrs Lewis in to join them. No sooner had everyone gone into the kitchen than there came another knock at the door. Buttons bounded up to the door closely followed by Mum, Dad, Winnie, Mrs Newnham, Percy, Edith and Mr and Mrs Lewis.

It was Mr Smith. He was holding his pot plant in his hands.

'Hello,' he said. 'My name is Mr Smith. Your little girl paid me a visit yesterday. She shared one of her Christmas crackers with me. It made me think how very peculiar it is that I've lived on this street for so long and yet I've never talked to you. So here I am to introduce myself and I've brought this for Winnie as a Christmas present.'

He handed her the pot plant. 'Plants need watering and fresh air and they also like to be talked to. Now that I know how very chatty and friendly you are, I'm sure you're the right person to look after it.'

Mum and Dad invited Mr Smith in to join everyone. It seemed unbelievable to Winnie that all these people who lived on the same street and never talked to each other were here, in her very house, drinking tea and eating mince pies and talking away merrily.

The little party was in full swing when, all of a sudden, there came a knock at the front door. Everyone gathered round the door to see who it was.

It was Old Granny Green Hat. Winnie could scarcely believe her eyes. She would never have suspected that Old Granny Green Hat would come over to their house after she had seemed rather grumpy with her.

'Hello,' said Old Granny Green Hat. 'Yesterday, your little girl came round my house to give me a Christmas cracker, and I just thought, well, I'd pop round and wish you all a Happy Christmas.' She gazed at the huge group of smiling people standing at the door. 'But I see now that you are having a Christmas party and I don't want to interrupt so I'll be on my way.'

'Oh no,' said Mum, 'don't feel you have to go, please do come and join us. We're having tea and mince pies, come on in! I'm Mrs Jones and well ... I'm sure you'll get to know who everyone is soon!'

'Oh,' said Old Granny Green Hat. 'Well, yes, my erm ... my name is erm ...' she looked at everyone smiling at her expectantly. 'Mrs Pritchard,' she said.

Hooray, thought Winnie. Finally, she knew the names of all her neighbours!

Mrs Pritchard stepped somewhat uncertainly inside the house. 'I don't want to bother anyone,' she said.

'Oh, it's no bother,' piped up Winnie. 'It's Christmas!'

In the midst of the jolly gathering Mum and Dad came up to Winnie and gave her a great big hug.

'Goodness me,' said Mum, 'what a busy day you had yesterday young lady! Now look what you've gone and done! All these people having fun in our home and it's all your fault!'

'Yes,' said Dad, 'not such a quiet street any more! Not since you've livened things up!'

Winnie felt so happy that she had brought everyone on the street together for a fun Christmas party. And all because she had wanted to share her Christmas crackers!

'I think,' said Mum, 'that you, Winnie, are just like a little cracker, full of surprises!'

'It wasn't just me,' said Winnie. 'Buttons helped.'

Buttons bounced up to Winnie and she hugged him tightly. It was such a wonderful morning and Winnie knew that from now on, people on the street would talk to each more often.

She had so much excitement bubbling up inside there was only one thing left to be said: 'Whoosh, whizz, pop, fizz, bang, crack!'

And so, that's the end of this story that wasn't quite a fairy tale but still filled everyone's lives with magic, once upon a time.

Also from The History Press

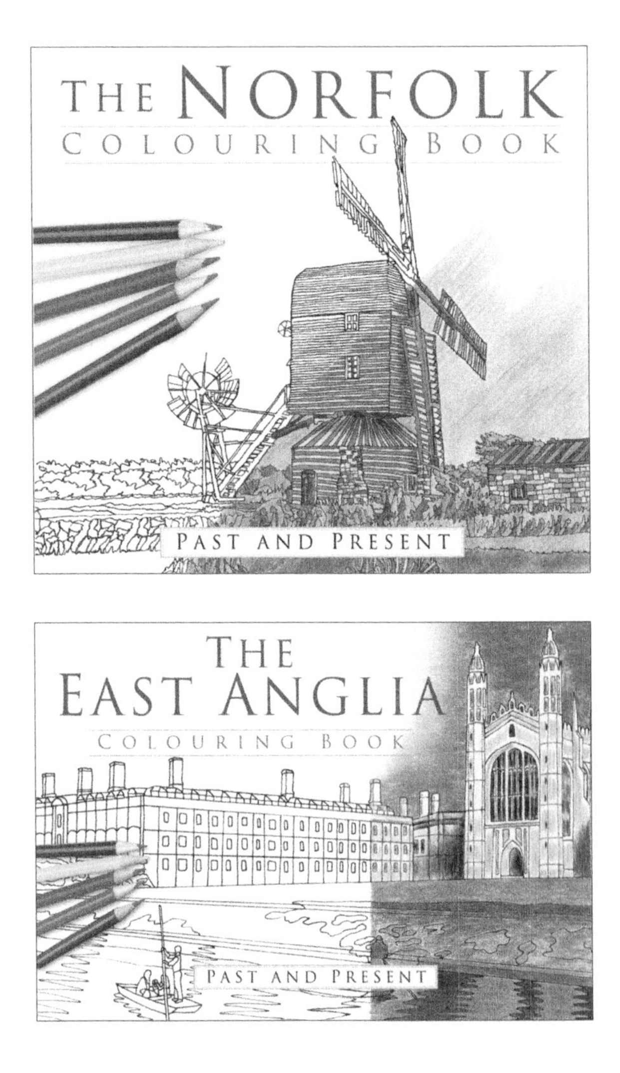